The Dark Knight of Assisi

William Baer

Southwell Press

The Dark Knight of Assisi / by William Baer

ISBN: 978-1-956199-05-5

Library of Congress Control Number: 2025907743

Cover Image: *Ghostly Figure with Medieval Sword* (shutterstock)

Cover Design: WB & Vanessa Jaramillo

Southwell Press, Wayne, New Jersey

southwellpress.com

for my family and friends

"But who are you, so foul and hopelessly lost?"
"I'm the one," he cried, "who weeps forever."
– Dante (*Inferno*, VIII, 35-36)

Chapter 1

Acre

May 18th, 1291

In the belltower of San Domenico, the young boy known as Visco sat high above the ravaged city in the Venetian Quarter. A curved Saracen dagger was resting in his lap, and the blood on its blade was still moist. For most of the day, he'd watched the merciless slaughter of the Christians at the breached walls of the city, then down below on the streets of Acre. He'd already accepted the fact, as well as a seven-year-old boy was capable, that he'd soon be dead, and even now, he could hear the heathens ransacking the House of God beneath him.

Strangely, he could hear angelic voices singing *"Salve Regina."* He glanced down past the flaming arsenal to the steps of San Paulo, where he saw a small group of Dominican nuns awaiting martyrdom with hymns of praise. They wouldn't have long to wait. At first, the boy wished that the sisters would run for their lives, even though it would have been useless, but mostly he admired their courage.

Their piety.

Almost immediately, a group of white-robed Saracen horsemen bore down on the nuns with long Egyptian swords and cut them to pieces, yet young Visco Malavolti never averted his eyes. He'd already seen too much cruelty today, and he'd become insensate to the violence. He was actually grateful that the good sisters were only slaughtered, since rape in the open streets had been common for hours.

Acre, the spectacular City of Churches, the richest city in the region, and the last major outpost of Christendom had been relentlessly annihilated before the child's eyes. He remembered that his Templar uncle and guardian, Augustus Damiano, had once told him that a Pharaoh named Thutose II had once captured the city fifteen hundred years before the birth of Christ, and now, today, the child had watched in horror as the forces of the Egyptians, under Sultan al-Ashraf Khalil, had once again decimated the jewel of the Palestinian coast.

Throughout the course of this terrible day, the young boy often found himself thinking about the dead and decomposing corpse of Sultan Qalawan, presently lying, since last year, in his palace in Cairo. Qalawan had instructed his son not to bury his body until Acre had fallen and every Christian "infidel" had been exterminated or driven into the sea. His dutiful son, al-Ashraf Khalil, had renewed his father's long campaign with a vengeance, and the rotted corpse of Qalawan would certainly be buried after today's decimation of the city.

Before his death, Qalawan had swept into Palestine, taken the Hospitaller fortress at Marqub, and two years ago, demolished Tripoli. Now his son, al-Ashraf Khalil, attended by his huge harems, had finally come to Acre with a *jihad* army that was truly breathtaking in its scope and capabilities. He had at his command over 200,000 Mameluke warriors, including 50,000 horsemen, supported by the greatest siege train in the known history of the world, including a hundred black-oxen *Mangonel* hurling machines and a hundred *Trebuchet* catapults.

The siege of Acre had begun thirty-three days ago, and bit by bit the concentric walls and towers of the great city had succumbed to the followers of Islam. First the English Tower fell, then the towers of Blois and St. Nicholas, then finally, three days ago, the Tower of King Henry II. Visco had watched as King Henry of Cyprus fought selflessly, courageously, at his doomed tower, as the valiant Templars tried, in vain, to reinforce the failing position of the Knights of the Hospital.

Early this morning, before dawn, the final bombardment began. Saracen catapults rained stones and incendiary missiles of Greek fire all over the city, as the inextinguishable flames raced across the tops of Acre's countless roofs and terraces, lighting up the fading night-sky. Everyone in Acre was aware that the final assault was about to begin, and everyone waited in silence, staring over the walls into the vague morning mist. Eventually, the morning silence was shattered by an invisible terrifying cacophony, as three hundred Mohammedans mounted on camels rumbled their kettledrums beneath the frenzied cries of the dervishes, the blasts of trumpets, and the incessant crashing of Egyptian cymbals.

From within the eerie half-light just before dawn, they suddenly emerged from the mist, racing through the Almond groves like demons from hell. They were led by white-robed screaming dervishes waving their flashing long knives, inciting the rest forward, as the 200,000 followed. In the vanguard were endless regiments of infantry led by white-turbaned *Emirs* and *Mullahs*. Then the elite Saracen horsemen. The ground trembled, the skies rained with arrows, and fire was everywhere, as the walls and towers of the city were collapsed by Saracen engineers, then breached by Islamic suicide squads.

Undaunted, the city's 800 knights and 12,000 soldiers fought back with amazing courage against impossible odds. They were led by young King Henry; Guillaume de Beaujeu, Grand Master of the Temple; Matthew of Clermont, Master of the Hospital; and the Swiss knight Otto of Grandson. After an insanely brutal and desperate battle at the Accursed Tower, the city's key fortification, Visco was certain that William, Matthew, and Otto were now dead.

The boy had watched everything from his place in the belltower. He'd seen the Grand Master, a man who'd always been especially kind to young Visco, fall from an arrow, probably poisoned, that impaled his neck. At that exact moment, the young boy knew that everything was lost, and he watched in vain for a glimpse of his uncle Augustus, the most awesome of mighty Templars, but he never actually saw him.

Surely Augustus was dead as well.

When the Accursed Tower was lost, fresh Saracen riders swept through the breach, and the sack of the city and the slaughter of the women and children began. Visco soon learned that nothing was impossible in this world as he watched in horror as Christian babies were cut in half, as pregnant young women were violated then sliced open while they were still alive.

Maybe the most pathetic sight was the terrible panic of the refugees at the Acre docks, where the last surviving Christians desperately tried to board the few remaining Venetian ships for passage to Cyprus. The evacuation was made even more chaotic by the tumultuousness of the raging sea and the cupidity of some of the so-called Christians. With particular disgust, Visco watched as Peter of Flor, a Catalan knight who'd fought bravely with the Templars just a few days earlier, extorted jewels and coins from frantic women who offered him everything they possessed for passage on a ship he'd illegally commandeered to make a quick fortune.

Earlier this afternoon, King Henry, as he was obliged to do, reluctantly left the hopeless city, and he was now safely at sea. But Patriarch Nicholas of Hanape, who'd generously allowed a number of desperate swimmers refuge on his small craft, was subsequently drowned when his small boat was swamped. Visco had watched in disbelief as the old man, almost instantly, disappeared beneath the tempestuous waves.

Now the docks were mostly empty, except for a few Saracen horsemen "riding down" an occasional stray Christian. Only a few insignificant vessels remained off the coast, as most of the great ships had already sailed from sight. Visco was supposed to have sailed early this morning, but he'd disobeyed his uncle and stayed. He wanted, above all, to be close to Augustus whom he loved like a father, and he also wanted to learn the fate of his actual father, Cesare Malavolti, an Assisian diplomat who'd been in Tripoli around the time of the city's siege and capture by the Egyptian Mamluks two years earlier.

Since everyone in Tripoli had been slaughtered, it was naturally assumed that his father was already dead, which Augustus had verified two years ago. But recently, six weeks ago, Visco had heard a rumor that his father had actually been murdered *before* the siege of Tripoli began. By a Christian knight. Unfortunately, before Visco could ask his uncle about it, Augustus had been sent by the Grand Master to Tortosa to gather more knights for the defense of Acre. Then, on the same day that Augustus returned from Tortosa with a hundred Templars, the siege of Acre initiated, and the boy hadn't seen his uncle since the knight's return to the city.

Nevertheless, despite relentless Saracen assaults, Augustus had arranged, through the friars at San Domenico, for the boy's safe passage to Cyprus for early this morning, but when the time had come, Visco hid himself in the Pisan Quarter until the ship disembarked. Then he went to his special place in the belltower. Somehow, in the course of the morning's fighting, Augustus had learned that the boy was still in Acre, and he'd sent a message through Friar Andreas to "wait at the bells." So Visco waited. Then a second message came that Augustus would try to arrive around 6:00, but it was already 6:30, and the boy was certain that his uncle was already dead, lying somewhere in the smoking ruins of the Accursed Tower.

He heard a piercing cry.

He looked down to the streets near St. Andrew's. The ravaging Saracens had discovered a young Christian girl hiding near the toppled Arch of Constantine. They immediately ripped the clothes from her body, as she cried out desperately, uselessly. Repulsed, the young boy looked away. He'd seen the workings of hell in Acre today, and he'd been numbed by everything that he'd seen, but he couldn't watch the young woman's violation. Instead, he stared down at the knife in his hands, which he'd pulled from the back of a dead Genoese trader during an earlier excursion down to the streets of Acre. He hated to disturb the poor man's corpse, but he felt that, when the time came, he should go to his death fighting.

Like his uncle Augustus.

Now it was time.

Visco stood up and vowed to kill at least one of the heathens before his death, so he could die like a Templar.

Then he was startled by a noise from below.

Someone, quickly, was coming up the belltower ladders, and it definitely wasn't Friar Andreas. Visco's heart surged in his chest, but he managed to keep his mind strangely calm. He stepped back into one of the tower's shadowed recesses, and he watched as a lean and powerful Saracen warrior rose through the trapdoor, went to the westside window, and immediately stepped onto the outside ledge. Then, very skillfully, he climbed to the top of the tower and was soon out of sight. The Muslim soldier had moved so quickly that Visco had held his place right where he was, attempting nothing.

Then the boy could hear loud banging from above, and he could see chunks of stone masonry falling from the belltower roof. He knew exactly what was happening. The Mohammedan was smashing the Christian cross off the top of the tower. He probably had a yellow Saracen flag concealed beneath his robes. Everywhere in the devastated city, the cross had been supplanted by the crescent.

As he waited, Visco prepared himself.

Quietly, he lifted one of the long wooden poles used to clean the huge brass bells. Then he stood patiently near the open window where the Saracen had climbed outside. The belltower had open windows on all four sides, but Visco was hopeful that the Muslim would come down from the roof the same way that he'd gone up. Finally, he could hear the man climbing back down.

At first, the boy could only see the Mameluke's dangling feet, but then the man dropped to the outside ledge facing into the tower. As soon as he did so, Visco thrust forward, striking the warrior heavily in the chest with the end of the bell-pole, knocking him backwards. Instantly, the man fell from sight, and the boy, both gratified and horrified by what he'd done, gasped for air and dropped the heavy pole.

Eventually, he walked over to the window and looked down into the seemingly possessed black eyes of the Saracen warrior. The falling man had somehow managed to grasp the sloping overhang just beneath the tower window. His fixed dark eyes were flush with hate, with arrogance. Even amusement. The Saracen had no doubt that he could quickly climb up from the overhang, enter the belltower, and kill the boy exactly as he pleased. Stunned, Visco instinctively backed away from the window. Briefly, he considered trying to assault the man with the bell-pole again, then he decided to go downstairs and die within the cathedral.

He grabbed his dagger, exited quickly through the trapdoor, and made a hasty descent down the long ladders and staircases into the sacristy of the cathedral. Everything was eerily quiet, but up above, Visco could see the distant form of the Saracen emerging through the trapdoor. Convinced that he only had a few moments to live, Visco decided that he wouldn't waste time attempting to run away or attempting to hide. Both ideas were useless. Nevertheless, he felt oddly calm, oddly resolved. He gripped his knife and walked into the church proper.

Maybe the child shouldn't have been astonished by what lay before him, but he was. Everything had been destroyed and desecrated: the altars, the stained-glass windows, the statuary. Even the pews had been smashed and torched. Then Visco saw a dead body lying in the apse, and he had no doubt that it was Friar Andreas. He walked over and stared down at the corpse. It was headless. Horrified, he looked around the church. Then he saw the friar's decapitated head sitting on the main altar in a pool of blood.

For some reason, the young boy lifted his eyes and stared at the only thing in the church not yet destroyed: the huge Byzantine "Christ Transfigured," which was painted on the interior roof over the main altar. It was a powerful and mesmerizing Christ, and the boy realized for the first time that he would be dying for Jesus Christ. The Muslims would kill him simply because he was an "infidel," and he wondered if he would be brave enough.

Then he was startled by a commotion at the open doors of the cathedral. Two Saracen soldiers rushed into the building, racing towards him. The boy lifted his knife, braced himself, but inexplicably the Mohammedans ran past him, as if fleeing something. Or someone. Then Visco heard an approaching horse, and he saw the huge form of a Templar, with the bright red cross emblazoned across the front of his white tunic. The knight rode his powerful white charger into the nave of the cathedral. The boy had never seen anything so magnificent in his whole life. It was his uncle, Augustus Damiano.

At the same moment, the Saracen from the belltower entered the cathedral and rushed towards the boy with his long knife. Seeing what was happening, Augustus spurred his stallion down the center aisle of the cathedral. When the Muslim saw that the Templar was riding towards him, he deftly hopped onto an overturned pew and leapt through the air at the racing horseman. In a single motion, the red-cross knight deflected the Saracen's weapon, drove his own dagger into the man's neck, then tossed his still bleeding corpse to the floor of the cathedral.

Without hesitation, the Templar continued riding directly toward the young boy, who understood his purpose. Visco held up his right arm. Then, as Augustus rode past, he leaned down, grabbed the boy by the arm, and powerfully lifted him off the ground, swinging him behind him on his charger. Quickly, he guided his mount past the altar, through the sacristy, and out the opened rear exit of the cathedral. The young boy held so tightly to his uncle's waist that he could barely see anything, but he did notice that Augustus bowed his head as he passed the altar.

With the boy holding from behind, the Templar rode his stallion halfway down the long esplanade behind San Domenico, where he pulled up his horse, lifted the boy down, and dismounted. All the time, Augustus was staring down at the sea which lay about two hundred feet beneath them in a sheer drop over the edge of the esplanade. Although the boy didn't fully comprehend his uncle's preoccupations, he noticed for the first time the extent of his uncle's wounds. His right thigh had been gashed open, and there was a Saracen arrow sticking out from the Templar's left shoulder. The bolt had clearly penetrated the knight's mail hauberk, and there were countless other cuts, bruises, and bloodstains everywhere on the man's battered body.

Augustus turned and looked down at the young boy.

"You disobeyed me, Visco."

The boy looked up at his uncle.

Augustus was the most powerful of the elite Templars. He was also the tallest man that Visco had ever seen from the Italian peninsula. He had powerful hands and shoulders, dark Sicilian hair, and a kindly, rugged, and handsome face. He was oddly clean-shaven, with unexpectedly clear blue eyes. Even the purple scar in the form of a cross that had been sliced into his forehead by a band of Islamic warriors only added to the mystique that surrounded the legendary Templar.

Augustus was only fifteen years older than Visco, but he seemed like a man far more experienced in the ways of the world than other men who were twice his age.

He was, in truth, everything that Visco aspired to be.

The boy responded.

"Yes."

The knight didn't bother to reprimand his nephew, and he even smiled at the boy's recklessness.

"Well, you're still alive," he decided. "Thank God for that."

Then the Templar sat down on the stone ledge that marked the edge of the esplanade where it dropped off to the sea, turning his left shoulder to the boy.

"Break it off."

Although extremely wary of the precipice, Visco did as he was told. With both hands, he grabbed the arrow, concentrated, then tried to snap the shaft. But it didn't work. He knew that his failed attempt must have hurt his uncle a great deal, but Augustus didn't complain.

"Try again," he said calmly, "you can do it, Visco."

Resolved, the young boy tightened his grip, concentrated harder, and tried again with all his strength. Finally, the shaft snapped about two inches from his uncle's shoulder.

"Good," Augustus said as he stood up again, quickly removing his red-cross tunic and his heavy mail hauberk, carefully sliding them over the remaining shaft of the arrow.

"Was my father murdered?" the boy asked.

Augustus was surprised, but he was forthright.

"Yes."

"By whom?"

"It's uncertain, Visco, but I'll find out eventually."

There was no reason to ask Augustus if he was certain. Visco knew that his uncle would never tell him such a thing if he wasn't positive.

"Why didn't you tell me two years ago?"

"You had enough to deal with."

The boy understood, but he was still confused, and he sat down on the ground away from the precipice. He was surprised to find that he had so little reaction to the confirmation of his father's murder. Maybe, on a day like today, he had no sorrow left. Or maybe it was because he really didn't know his father very well. His father was always gone, never having much time for his only son. His only child. So the boy, motherless and now fatherless, remained strangely ambivalent.

Then he heard a dervish's cry.

They'd been spotted by a white-robed fanatic who was now rushing down the long esplanade towards them. At the same moment, a Muslim horseman came riding through the back door of the cathedral, heard the dervish's cry, and also began racing towards Augustus. Suddenly, all of Visco's comforting numbness was gone. The deadening effect of the day's massacres vanished, and his natural fears returned with a fury. Even the awesome presence of his uncle, which had recently given the boy hope again, seemed inadequate in their desperate situation, as the two Muslim warriors bore down on them.

Visco was more terrified than he'd been all day.

As always, Augustus remained calm, almost inhumanly calm, and the boy wondered if the knight had already accepted his inevitable martyrdom right here on the Acre esplanade. But if that was true, then why did he take off his red-cross tunic?

"What's this?" the Templar asked as he bent over the boy and picked up the Saracen dagger. Visco was too frightened to respond. The dervish, with his long raised knife, was almost upon them, but Augustus calmly took the time to examine Visco's knife, even wasting a moment to balance it in his palm. Satisfied, he turned around to face the charging Muslim who was only a few paces away. Suddenly, the Templar lifted up the dagger and flung it, quick as an arrow shaft, into the man's chest. The knife sunk all the way down to the hilt with a tremendous sickening thud. The dying dervish screeched loudly in the twilight, collapsing to his death at the feet of Templar.

Then Augustus picked up his own huge sword and faced the charging horseman. Augustus's weapon was a long "hand-and-a-half" sword with a double-tapered blade, with a beautiful cross pommel. He held his weapon horizontally at his waist and waited motionlessly for the Saracen rider. The Mameluke was riding a tremendous white mount, holding a long curved sword over his head. He seemed perfectly invincible as he bore down on a dismounted, wounded, unmailed knight with an extremely heavy sword.

Horrified, Visco attempted to look away, but he couldn't.

At the last possible moment, Augustus stepped to his right, and with a powerful uppercut of his long heavy sword struck the horse deep into the side of its neck. Immediately, the dead horse tumbled to a heap, throwing its rider, and knocking down the Templar as well. With remarkable agility, the Saracen warrior weathered the fall and quickly sprang to his feet. In a few breathless seconds, he was standing over the now kneeling knight holding his curved sword high in the air.

"No!" the boy cried out.

Uselessly.

Before the weapon came down, Augustus, with a powerful sweep of his sword, slashed into the Saracen's left knee, almost separating, in a gush of blood, the man's thigh from his lower leg. Instantly, the Muslim collapsed to the ground, bleeding to death, and Visco was grateful that he couldn't see the dying man's face.

As Augustus rose from his knees, several more Saracen soldiers exited from the cathedral and started rushing towards them. Once again, the boy despaired. There seemed to be no end to the heathens, but the Templar knight, who glanced over his shoulder, seemed unfazed.

Then the Templar stepped to the edge of the precipice, faced the sea, and kissed the cross hilt of his sword. Then he tossed his red-crossed tunic down to the waters below and held his sword at his side.

"Stand up, Visco," he said.

The boy did as he was told.

"Come over here."

Warily, the boy approached the edge of the esplanade. As he did so, he saw a small craft, a rowboat of some kind, bobbing in the tempestuous waters far beneath them. When he understood his uncle's intentions, he was terrified.

"I can't," he whispered. "I can't!"

Gently, Augustus took the boy's face into his right hand and turned it upwards towards his own.

"You *can*, Visco, and you must."

The boy said nothing.

"You can do *anything*," the knight assured him.

Once again, Augustus looked over his shoulder. Visco could hear the Saracen cries bearing down upon them, but the powerful knight paused and bowed his head.

"Great God, forgive us our failures, remember our meager efforts in Your Holy Name." Then he whispered, "*Jesu Christe, Rex mundi!*"

Finally, the Templar took the boy's hand in his own.

Visco mustered his courage, and together they leapt over the edge of the escarpment and dropped like ballast for over two hundred feet into the turbulent, freezing Mediterranean.

The Crusades were over.

The great dream of *Outremer* was finished, and Al-Ashraf Khalil had been true to his vow. The entire city was now in his possession except for a surviving Templar fortress in the southwest corner of Acre. But even that battlement, despite reinforcements brought by Augustus, fell within the next ten days. Falling into a smoking heap of rubble. With the exception of the few who managed to escape to

Cyprus during the forty-three-day siege, every single inhabitant of Acre had been slaughtered or enslaved, and the entire city was decimated. Absolutely everything was destroyed, demolished, or burned: fortifications, churches, palaces, castles, houses, the harbor, the warehouses, the orchards, the vineyards, even the irrigation system.

In the aftermath of Acre, the few remaining coastal fortifications soon succumbed. Tyre was abandoned, Sidon and Haifa fell to the triumphant heathen, and the Templar castles at Tortosa and Athlit were also evacuated. As was Beirut. Soon nothing in the Middle East remained in Christian hands except the impregnable Templar fortress on the tiny and seemingly insignificant island of Ruad.

The fertile coast of Palestine had been methodically transformed into a wasteland. Every trace, every vestige, of the Christians and their culture had been eradicated with a maniacal vengeance. Captured Christians gutted the slave markets of the East, girls and women vanished into Saracen harems, and captured knights were enslaved in Egyptian galley ships. The *jihad* had triumphed, and now the rotting body of Qalawan could finally be buried in Cairo.

The Crusades were over.

Chapter 2

Malavolti

Montone, the Papal States: September 1319

Twenty-eight Years Later

The infantry scavengers heard him coming as they picked over the dead that littered the field before the Fortress of Montone. Malavolti emerged from the woods on his dark mount, followed by his young squire, Lorenzo Vasari. The scavengers knew who he was, of course, and they preferred not to look in his direction. His uncanny coldness and violent nature frightened them all and made them anxious. As they continued ransacking the freshly-dead for valuables, they casually moved away from the spot where the dark knight had paused his black charger in the midst of the field of death.

An hour earlier, the same mercenary knight, Visconte Malavolti, under the overall command of the German mercenary Berthold Oetker, had ambushed the forces of Parisio of Metola when the Capitano of Massa Trabaria had attempted to return to his temporary refuge. Within less than twenty minutes, all two hundred riders of Parisio's elite cavalry were dead, and a fair number of those now lying in the fields of Montone had fallen to the double-edged, tapered sword of the ferocious Malavolti.

In the aftermath of his stunning success, the mercenary knight was now surveying the field of battle. He was a tall, extremely powerful, extremely imposing figure, dressed only in black except for a small white *fleur-de-lis* high on the left chest of his black tunic, even though the great warrior looked far more Italian than French. His hair and his eyes were dark, as was his complexion, and his clean-shaven face was strikingly handsome in the rugged, military manner of the Umbrian knights. His features seemed almost regal, probably of noble blood, but his eyes were worn and old before their time. They'd either seen too much or suffered too much in the man's thirty-five years, and they looked eerily impassive, detached, and cold-blooded.

As the dark knight looked up at the gray skies, his squire drew closer with the bird and removed its hood. It was a rare and valuable peregrine with stunning plumage. It had been a gift to Malavolti from Robert the Bruce after the great Scottish victory at Bannockburn five years earlier. The falcon had originally been captured from the famous cliff-nests near Dunnottar Castle at Stonehaven, and it was later trained to hawk by the renowned Brabantine falconers of Flanders. The bird was so aggressive and audacious that it had been trained, upon special signal, to attack the face of a human being. It was the ultimate bird of prey, and certainly a fit gift from a great king to a valued mercenary.

"A heron," Lorenzo said with anticipation as he spotted the large bird leisurely rising above a cluster of oaks.

Malavolti had already spotted the heron, and he didn't bother to respond to his young squire. For a few moments, the emotionless knight watched as the unsuspecting prey soared, carefree, against the dark grey sky. Finally, he nodded to his squire, and Lorenzo cast off the bird from his left wrist into the wind.

"Prey!" the squire cried out enthusiastically.

Immediately, the distant heron sensed its mortal danger and began a magnificent spiraling flight upward into the heavens. But the much swifter Falcon, with its golden Milanese bells tinkling lightly as it rose, was instantly after it, pursuing the doomed bird with breathtaking upward gyrations into the dark afternoon sky. Eventually, the peregrine attained the loftier position, then instantly flung itself downward onto the wind until, with a brilliant final swoop, it crashed down on top of the helpless heron with a powerful blow of its sharp talons.

The hunt was over.

Malavolti was pleased.

The bird, which he loved, which he called Scone, dropped the dead heron in front of his charger before swooping back to its perch on Lorenzo's gloved arm.

"Well done!" said the young squire, wiping the blood from the peregrine's talons. Then he looked at his knight.

"Can it feed?"

Malavolti thought it over a moment and decided it was a good idea.

"Just the heart."

The eager squire nodded, dismounted, and began to cut open the warm heron with his knife.

Suddenly bored, Malavolti glanced over the field of death. He was sick of war. Not for sentimental reasons, but because it had provided him with so little that he really wanted. He'd been a warrior, in one capacity or another, for eighteen years, and yet he still had very little to show for it. His mercenary wages were perfectly reasonable, even fair, but Malavolti wanted more. *Much* more. Even the commendations of kings and commanders, as when Berthold had ridden onto the field thirty minutes ago and praised him lavishly in front of the troops, meant absolutely nothing to the dark knight.

He wanted wealth. *Great* wealth. It was plain and simple, and he wanted nothing else. All the other so-called pleasures of life had failed him over the years, and now he wanted to live out his life in comfort and luxury. Which was why he was here in Montone, fighting amid the absurd military squabbles of the Italian Papal States.

A trumpet sounded a single blast from the fortress, and Malavolti looked at a distant messenger who waved his right arm as he'd been instructed. The signal meant that Parisio, who'd barely survived the ambush, was conscious again. Malavolti was certain that the Capitano wouldn't last much longer, and that was exactly what he wanted. It was why he'd come to Montone in the first place: to make sure that his wealthy cousin Parisio was killed so he could make an immediate claim to the man's fortress and estates at Metola.

Before leaving the field, Malavolti glanced down at his falcon as it greedily tore at a bit of the heron's bloody heart. The dark knight, of course, was not impervious to the common literary analogy between a knight, especially a mercenary knight, and his bird of prey. In truth, Malavolti was not at all displeased that he and Scone had so much in common. When the peregrine was finished eating, Lorenzo looked up at his master, but Malavolti said nothing.

The dark knight wasn't quite sure what to make of his new young squire, barely sixteen, whom he'd taken on just two months ago after his longtime attendant, Parenzo Greca, was murdered in his bed by robbers in a tavern in Abruzzo. A few days later, Lorenzo Vasari arrived, claiming to be a distant bastard cousin on Malavolti's paternal side, which was hardly a recommendation. But the dark knight took him on, finding that the young boy was both competent and taciturn, which Malavolti appreciated, but also secretive and brooding. Whenever Malavolti had the time, he'd consider finding someone else.

He spurred his charger across the body-strewn field toward the fortress.

Eighteen years ago, when Malavolti was a much different young man in the service of the king of France, he'd been sent on a diplomatic mission to Florence with his mentor, Prince Rostand de Cornay. It was there in Florence, years ago, that Malavolti had acquired his first squire, the talented and always loyal Parenzo, and it was during that same mission that he'd briefly encountered his older cousin Parisio in Reggello. Unfortunately, his cousin was an insufferably vain and condescending man. It seemed that the man's vaunted reputation for military prowess was justified, but the Capitano of Massa Trabaria was a detestable self-absorbed man who repulsed the youthful Malavolti in every way possible.

His death would be a loss to no one.

Silently, Malavolti entered the death chamber and watched from across the room. He had no intention of making his presence known, although he didn't care one way or the other if Parisio learned that his own cousin had been the instrument of his death.

It made no difference.

As anticipated, Parisio was mostly delirious, mostly incoherent, but Malavolti was surprised to discover that the man was apparently racked with guilt.

"My child!" the Capitano called out desperately.

Malavolti was astonished. Parisio had no children, and his wife, Emilia, had died of a fever last year.

"Child! Forgive me!"

The restless warrior called out to no one in particular as a useless medic and an equally useless priest tried to comfort the dying man.

"May God forgive me for what I have done to my child!"

Malavolti's curiosity was naturally aroused, but he was repulsed by his cousin's behavior. The dark knight had no sympathy for a man like Parisio who'd been a smug atheist his entire life and was now pathetically calling out for mercy to the God he'd ridiculed.

Simply because death was waiting in the chamber.

Suddenly, Parisio looked up at the priest and grabbed the old man's forearm.

"Will God forgive me?"

"God forgives those," the priest responded, "who are truly sorry for their transgressions." Then he leaned over the man, "Would you like to confess?"

"Yes! Yes!"

But Parisio's strength was fading quickly.

Curious, Malavolti stepped forward, close to Parisio's bed, but his cousin slumped into unconsciousness. Undeterred, the dark knight leaned over the bed.

"What child?" he asked firmly.

There was no response.

Angry, the dark knight straightened up and glared at the priest.

"What child?" he repeated with intimidation.

"I have no idea."

"Are you attached to Parisio in any way?"

"No, I'm from Roccastrada."

Malavolti believed him.

Then he stared down at his pathetic cousin, and he understood.

"A bastard!" he thought to himself. Of course! Parisio's wife, Lady Emilia, was reputed to have been a very beautiful woman, but it's rare that a powerful man like Parisio can resist the peasant girls and the traders' daughters. Regardless, it meant nothing to Malavolti. A bastard would have no hereditary rights.

Satisfied, he left the room. In three days' time, he would arrive in Metola and make his claim to the fortress and its surrounding estates.

As fully expected, Parisio died within the hour. The next morning, Malavolti took his fee in gold from Berthold Oetker along with the dead body of his cousin.

Then he and Lorenzo left Montone.

Chapter 3

Maria Angelina

Near Niccone, the Papal States, September 1319

"**S**hould we do something?" Lorenzo asked.

A few minutes earlier, the dark knight had stopped on a high bluff so his squire could feed the falcon and check the corpse that was draped over the pack horse. As the boy attended to his chores, Malavolti sat on his charger and impassively watched as a robbery was taking place down below on the main thoroughfare. Three mounted highwaymen had commandeered a small carriage escorted by a Pisan soldier. In a matter of moments, the brigands had dispatched the soldier, and they were now extorting valuables from the passengers of the carriage.

Lorenzo, feeding Scone bits of dried meat, also watched the brigands, and he was aching for a fight. His master, however, seemed disinclined. The dark knight had other things on his mind.

Down on the roadway, two of the brigands had dismounted to check out the carriage more carefully, while a contentious elderly monk, who'd somehow exited the vehicle, was defiantly arguing with the still-mounted leader of the robbers.

Malavolti remained disinterested.

Besides, he detested Franciscans.

He finally responded to Lorenzo.

"I see no need."

Although he spoke with finality, Lorenzo didn't give up.

"There's a woman in the carriage, my lord."

At first, nothing registered on the face of Malavolti.

"Are you certain?"

"I am."

Malavolti stared at the open carriage door, but he could see nothing in the shadows. Finally, he made his decision.

"Kill the one threatening the priest," he said matter-of-factly.

Lorenzo nodded. He quickly tied down his mount and the pack horse, removed the arbalest from his saddle, and immediately ran down the sloping field, disappearing into a cluster of trees.

Malavolti watched him go with complete indifference. When the time was right, he drew out his huge sword and spurred his black charger down the dirt path that would eventually sweep around an intervening stand of trees and lead to the main road.

At the carriage, the frustrated leader of the brigands, a notorious highwayman named Octavian Turacco, had dismounted from his horse and forced his dagger to the throat of the defiant monk. The priest leaned back against the side of the carriage, but the brigand pressed forward, pressing his knife into the monk's neck, drawing a stream of blood. Inside the carriage, an unseen woman gasped, but the highwayman paid no attention, glaring into the monk's unrelenting eyes.

"Nothing would give me a greater pleasure, Franciscan," Turacco said, as the Franciscan fully expected to feel the man's blade slice deep into his throat.

"Where is it?" Turacco demanded.

"There's no more gold," the Franciscan replied firmly. "We've given you everything we have."

"I don't believe it!"

Turacco glanced into the carriage and saw the young lady's rings. She was wearing at least four, all of high value, and the brigand was furious at the incompetence of his accomplices.

"Give me those rings, girl," he called into the carriage, "or I'll slit this old man's throat."

Before the young woman could respond, Turacco heard the thundering sound of a horseman approaching at a full gallop from behind him. As he turned to look, his head jerked violently as a bolt burst three inches out of his chest. The arrow had entered into his back and sliced through his torso. Stunned, Turacco managed to turn around to see young Lorenzo emerging from the woods carrying his crossbow. The brigand collapsed in a heap.

At the same time, the other two thieves, who'd been ransacking a trunk behind the carriage, heard Turacco fall then turned to see the dark knight bearing down on them. At breathtaking speed. One of the men dove into the woods and managed to escape, but the other man ran for his horse and was immediately run down by Malavolti. The dark knight's blow was so swift that the man was probably dead before he felt the blade striking his shoulder.

He tumbled into the dirt in a pool of his own blood.

Satisfied, Malavolti rode back to the carriage where the monk was checking on the unseen occupants of the carriage. Then the old priest turned around to face the dark knight. The Franciscan was about sixty years old, still solid, still vigorous. He also had a deep purple scar across his left cheek.

"Bless you, young knight."

The priest's gratitude was obviously sincere, but the dark knight sensed the man's wariness. He had the uneasy feeling that the monk, a man he'd never seen before, had somehow "understood" him in some special way that Malavolti didn't want fathomed. Instinctively, he disliked the man and felt uneasy in his presence.

But something else was unsettling Malavolti, as if there was some kind of imminent danger lurking nearby. Ever since he'd been a young child, the dark knight had possessed a unique inexplicable sense of impending tragedy. Some of those who'd known him felt that it was the result of his childhood experiences during the fall of Acre, but Malavolti felt that it went back even further, to his own birth, when his mother had died.

Now the feeling was upon him again, but when he looked around, he saw nothing that concerned him.

Then the dark knight heard gentle sobbing from the interior of the carriage. When he looked to his right, he could see two women, a crying older attendant and a terrified young lady, who were trying to comfort each other. When the young girl looked up, directly at Malavolti, he saw her face for the first time, and he was stunned. He felt as if he'd been struck a deadly blow. As if his whole world, *everything*, everything that he'd ever been and everything that he presently was, had violently imploded.

He was overcome.

With rage, with exhilaration.

With affection, with abomination.

Chapter 4

Zampa

Niccone, the Papal States, September 1319

H e felt a sharp burn scorching his face.

It was the morning sun, but he kept his eyes closed.

Slowly, Malavolti woke from a restless sleeping hell into a far worse waking reality. He was still slightly drunk from the previous evening, and he was violently nauseated, and his whole body throbbed and ached.

Finally, despite the pain, the sickened knight sat up and looked around him. He was lying in an isolated field, seemingly alone, and covered with blood. The blood was mostly dried, but some of it was still damp, and he wondered if it was recent, or maybe the result of the morning dew. He also wondered if the blood was his own, but he wasn't sure. Despite his sickness, despite his pain, he couldn't feel any open wounds, and he naturally wondered what had happened.

Nearby, his black charger was waiting patiently for its master. Also nearby, was the pack horse with the slowly-rotting corpse of his cousin,

Parisio, draped over its back. Hanging from the same horse, he could see the covered cage of the peregrine. He was glad to see that his bird was all right.

Then he wondered about Lorenzo.

Gradually, he started coming to his senses, remembering bits of the night before. Then he spotted the body of the Franciscan monk, Salvatore Zampa, lying off to his right.

Obviously dead.

Then he remembered whatever he could remember.

After the encounter on the thoroughfare, he'd accompanied the young woman, Maria Angelina Sorella, and her two companions to an inn near Niccone. Deciding to spend the night, he'd joined the young woman, her attendant Leonora, and the monk Zampa for a late meal at the inn.

Within these rememberings, Malavolti refused to recollect the extent of the young girl's beauty, or her unaffected grace, but he did remember that she was the youngest daughter of a wealthy Pisan noble, Enrico Sorella, and that she was returning to Pisa from Macerata where she'd been nursing a sick relative. Her three older sisters had all been properly married, each carefully matched by their parents, and now Maria, age fifteen, had been betrothed to an older Genoese nobleman whom she'd only met once in her life, for less than an hour.

During the meal, the girl was polite, charming, but mostly quiet. She was clearly a pious young woman, and despite the harsh experiences of the afternoon and her naturally shy demeanor, Malavolti discerned a playful aspect in the young girl that wrenched his heart and checked his appetite.

Despite his best efforts, the dark knight recalled the young girl's remarkable beauty: her thick brown hair decorated with pink flowers, the thoughtful brown eyes, the perfect angelic features. Her only vanity seemed to be her numerous finger rings which, despite their value and bright sparkle, seemed lost amid the girl's breathtaking beauty.

As discretely as possible, Malavolti had watched the girl's every movement during their meal together, and when she retired for the evening with her attendant, he was overcome with a powerful confusion of violent emotions. To distract himself, he drank more red wine with the friendly monk, who was, as Malavolti had assumed, not a typical Franciscan.

Zampa had been born in Spoleto. Like Saint Francis himself, he was the son of a merchant, became a soldier, then became a monk. But Zampa, who would never have approved of the comparison, had a longer and more gradual path to Holy Orders. When he finally abandoned warfare for the cross, he found himself aligning with the so-called "Spiritual" Franciscans in their struggles to keep the order simple and poor. But Salvatore Zampa was neither a radical nor a dogmatic, and he supported the great compromise initiated by Bonaventure which favored the more numerous "Moderate" Franciscans and eventually allowed for the order's property and wealth to be held in corporate ownership by the papacy.

Nevertheless, Zampa had been horrified by the Vatican bull of the previous year, *Gloriosam Ecclesiam*, which declared the Spirituals in heresy, eventually leading to their excommunication. With difficulty, Zampa had accepted the challenge of humbling himself and silently following the order. He was now centered at the Monastery of San

Giuseppe near Pisa, and, since he was distantly related to the Sorellas, he'd become the young girl's confessor. When he and Malavolti had been drinking much too much for much too long, the priest had laughed at the irony of his situation.

"I'm confessor to someone who had no sins!"

Throughout the evening, the old monk kept a small wooden cross pressed firmly in his left hand, probably as a reminder of his spiritual obligations. Nevertheless, he was independent and outspoken, as well-versed in warfare as theology, with a marked taste for secular poetry, especially Cavalcanti and the Ravennan exile. The old habits had clearly died hard in Salvatore Zampa, and he was still a bit of a man of action who liked his wine more than he should. But his flaws, if that's what they were, seemed few and insignificant, and throughout their long evening together, Malavolti kept thinking to himself, "This clever monk is too damned smart for his own good. Not to mention, too damned good."

During their conversations, Malavolti refrained from revealing too much about himself, especially since he felt, as he had earlier on the thoroughfare, that the monk had somehow "understood" him, which made the dark knight extremely cautious and wary. He also refrained from asking any direct questions about the young girl Maria, but he paid close attention to any references that the monk made to his "most favorite child."

Then things grew rather hazy in the disordered mind of the dark knight. He could vaguely remember getting too drunk, something he never did. He also remembered trying to resist his attraction to the young girl who was now sleeping in her room. Finally, he convinced himself that he should leave the inn as soon as possible. When the monk retired for the evening, Malavolti went looking for Lorenzo to prepare the horses, but he couldn't remember anything that happened after that.

With the morning sun proving unbearable, Malavolti, with difficulty, stood up in the strange field. He glanced at his charger, and the horse immediately came to his side. Then he noticed, off in the distance near a stone wall, the dead body of his young squire. He walked over and looked down at the corpse. The boy's head was distorted, as if crushed against the wall.

He stared at the boy, but he felt nothing. Maybe a bit of sadness, nothing more. He wondered briefly if he was deranged in some way.

What was wrong with him?

What had he become?

Then, in a rush, he remembered the girl in the garden under the stars. Then lying on the ground. He suddenly realized what he had done, and he was shocked. He also knew that he had killed both the boy and the priest.

He was overcome.

Overwhelmed with a debilitating wave of horror and self-revulsion.

For a moment, he considered taking the dagger from his belt and thrusting it into his heart. His self-hatred was so powerful that he rocked on his feet and needed to hold onto his mount. Eventually, gradually, with a force of the will, the dark knight regained control of himself.

"So *that's* what I've become," he said to himself before he forced it from his mind.

All of it.

Which was something he'd trained himself to do ever since he was a young boy.

Then Malavolti mounted his black charger, retrieved the pack horse with his rotting cousin, and left for Mengara.

Never once did he look back at the dead behind him.

Chapter 5

Craxi

"Let's wait for a squirrel," the old professor suggested.

Malavolti didn't mind. Besides it wouldn't take long, the Roman ruins were overrun with the little creatures. Almost immediately, a curious brown squirrel appeared at the base of the eastern wall, and Craxi ignited the cloth-strip and stepped back beside the dark knight. Together, along with Craxi's three assistant-pupils, they watched as the flame swiftly glided across the ground toward the petard.

The explosion was tremendous. The delighted old man covered his ears, and his students cheered with excitement. The wall collapsed in a heap, and the ground shook beneath them. When the dust started to settle, Craxi looked up at Malavolti in amazement. Then he stepped towards the rubble and poked at the scattered remains of the squirrel with a wooden stick.

Malavolti said nothing. He was fully prepared to let the old scientist be a scientist, but he wasn't as pleased as the old man. Such an explosion might blow a single soldier to pieces, but it would take a lot more to breach a castle wall.

Craxi returned.

"You need," Malavolti pointed out, "to bind the halves of the grenade even tighter. Also, increase the percentage of charcoal to sulfur."

"I will!" the old man assured him. "I will! Now, let's go inside."

The dark knight nodded and followed the aged professor into his laboratory, as the old man's three assistants, knowing their place, waited outside.

Malavolti had picked Craxi very carefully, but he'd done so only by reputation. Now that he'd met the man in person, he was pleased with his choice. The old scientist was at least seventy years old, but he was still ambitious, and he clearly had enough life in him to finish the initial stages of the project. He was definitely brilliant enough, having studied at Bologna and taught at Paris. Like Roger Bacon, whom he'd known during an apprenticeship in London, Craxi was a believer not only in theoretical and speculative genius, but in the proofs of the laboratory.

Inside the small stone workhouse, Malavolti was gratified to see the tools of the old man's profession: furnaces, chemicals, metals, beakers, scales, drawings, and all kinds of precision implements. When the old man sat in his small chair, appropriate to his diminutive stature, he looked up at Malavolti and wasted no time.

"What do you want from me, young knight?"

"I want you to make us both rich," said the dark knight, "and to make you immortal. I have no interest in such things."

Malavolti was serious, but the old man smiled craftily.

"I've only got a few years left, young lord, so you'll have to convince me that I should spend it fooling around with saltpetre explosions."

Malavolti considered how he should initiate his argument.

"Do you have an understanding of warfare, old man?"

"I understand many things in this life, but not that. I've led a scholar's life."

Malavolti nodded.

"That's no concern, besides, most kings and knights have no real understanding of the essentials of warfare, which frequently leaves them dead in distant lands."

"Help me understand."

Malavolti pulled a table near the fireplace and sat down on top of it. He was in no rush. It was a few hours ride to Metola, and he didn't plan to arrive at the castle until early tomorrow morning. Besides, a bit of "war talk" might distract him from other things.

"It might surprise you to learn that the course of warfare is on the verge of altering itself dramatically, yet only a handful of the military leaders in Europe are aware of what's happening, even though the seeds of this alteration were sown at Courtrai over fifteen years ago."

"Were *you* at Courtrai?"

"I was," Malavolti remembered, "and I was like all the other young French cavalry knights: presumptuous, convinced of our invincibility, and foolish beyond reason. When Philip decided to punish the resistance in Flanders, I eagerly followed Robert of Artois into the lowlands. We had a huge army, over 7,000 highly skilled horse with nearly 30,000 foot. Robert, of course, like all good knights, despised the infantry, and he was fond of pronouncing in his bellicose way, 'A hundred horse is worth a thousand foot.'"

Then Malavolti realized something.

"Weren't you teaching in Paris at the time?"

"I was, but I remember very little about Courtrai, except for the aftermath."

Malavolti continued.

"The Flemish forces, under Guy de Namur, took up an excellent position beyond the marshes to confront the inevitable cavalry charge, and they massed a huge block of over 10,000 infantry armed with steel hats, gambesons, and a peculiar Flemish pike called a goedendag. To Robert of Artois and the rest of the elite French cavalry, they appeared as nothing more than pathetic prey, so after a perfunctory rain of arrows, Robert gave the signal, and the first wave of ten heavy squadrons charged forward. To our astonishment, the Flemish pha-lanx responded by boldly pressing forward into the charging French knights, bottling them up on the marshy ground, then cutting them to pieces with their goedendags, which had a club-like shaft designed for knocking riders from their saddles and a sharp spike protruding from the top to dispatch the fallen cavalry.

"It was a horrible massacre. I was only eighteen at the time, and I was waiting and watching in one of the rear cavalry squadrons, but we were never able to move forward and join the battle. Soon we were called to retreat, and most of the French army left the lowlands with-out seeing action. Robert, despite begging for quarter, got his brains bashed out by the detested bourgeoisie, and over 700 pairs of knightly spurs were later hung in the high church at Courtrai by the victorious Flemish. Nevertheless, the moronic French noblesse absolutely refused to acknowledge the truth about Courtrai, as every possible excuse was mustered to rationalize the defeat: the marsh, miscommunication, cowardice, and anything else they could conjure up. Anything but the truth."

"What *was* the truth, young knight?"

"That a thousand years of cavalry supremacy had come to an end in the marshy fields of Flanders. That the days of the armored knight are numbered. That the infantry is coming."

Malavolti paused, then continued.

"Much the same thing happened more recently, five years ago, at Bannockburn under the brilliant Scot, Robert the Bruce. His fearless infantry, supported by a well-timed cavalry charge, destroyed the elite of the English baronage. Over a thousand of King Edward's earls, barons, and knights were slaughtered that day, being the worst massacre of English peerage in the country's history."

"Were you at Bannockburn as well?" Craxi asked in amazement.

"I was. It was during my exile, and I can assure you, without a doubt, that the infantry of the future will not only dominate the field, it will do so supported with the yeoman's longbow."

The old man was astonished.

"The Roman phalanx," Malavolti continued, "gave way to barbarian light-riders about a thousand years ago at Adrianople, and ever since Charles Martel and Charlemagne, heavy-armored riders have reigned supreme, but it's coming to an end."

Even though it was difficult for Craxi to believe, the old professor was certainly willing to consider the possibility, but he was still missing something.

"But what's all that got to do with explosions? With black-powder?"

"Explosions, if they're powerful enough will end the efficacy of stone fortresses. Then castles will be as antiquated as armored cavalry. Maybe even sooner. And whoever supplies wall-breaching grenades to the royal courts of Europe will become rich beyond anyone's imagining, and that's only the beginning."

The old professor was clearly spellbound by the dark knight's visionary speculations.

"If that's only the beginning," he wondered, "what's the end?"

"It would take an imaginative mind like yours to comprehend it," Malavolti warned him.

"I'm willing to try."

"Everyone likes a big bang," the dark knight explained, "and simple-minded men have been intrigued by the flash and pop of black-powder ever since your old friend Roger Bacon conjured a workable sulfur/charcoal/saltpetre combination in *Epistolae de Secretis Operibus*. For dramatic effect, Bacon's concoction even superseded the mysterious Greek fire of the Saracens, which was only an incendiary, not an explosive.

"The subsequent emphasis on the blast of the saltpetre has proceeded at a rapid pace, especially after Marcus Graecus's recipes in *Liber Ignium*. I've seen impressive demonstrations of its power all across the continent, just as we did earlier in the ruins outside. But, in truth, it's only child's play.

"The *true* revolutionary power of saltpetre compounds lies in their propulsive capacities. Right now, even as we speak, certain sophisticated weapons-masters in various parts of the Italian peninsula are constructing large *vasi* to fire huge projectiles over, as well as through, fortress walls. Such weaponry could also be used to scatter infantry masses, and the French are working on a number of similar projects which they call *pots de fer*."

Malavolti stopped, then stared down at the intent little professor.

"There's money in this, old man, but immortality as well."

The dark knight rose from the table, picked up a charcoal implement, and made a few steady markings on a loose parchment.

"I've been carrying this figure in my head for over three years, ever since I first conceived the idea on a battlefield in Bohemia, and I've told absolutely no one."

Malavolti paused, then glared down into the eager eyes of the little professor, warning him bluntly.

"Secrecy insures your life, old man. Nothing else."

Craxi understood, quickly nodding his agreement.

"I'm no stranger to secrets," he assured the dark knight.

Satisfied, Malavolti laid the parchment in the old man's lap. Craxi lifted it up to his eyes, and he was stunned by the simplicity of the diagram: an iron tube clamped to a wooden stock of some kind, with a touchhole for ignition. All of it less than a foot long.

Amazed, Craxi looked up at Malavolti.

"A weapon for the hand? A portable *vasi* for every footman in Europe?"

The dark knight said nothing, allowing Craxi to think about it for a few moments. Then Malavolti asked the crucial question.

"Can you do it?"

"Yes."

He spoke with conviction, with enthusiasm.

Then Malavolti bent over, picked up the parchment, and tossed it into the fireplace. After a moment's hesitation, it ignited into a flash of flames and turned to black.

Malavolti returned his attention to the old scientist.

"How soon can it be done?"

"I'll need resources," he explained. "Despite my scholarly reputation, I'm a man of modest means."

Malavolti knew that it was true.

Without a word, he lifted a heavy pouch from his belt and dropped it with a loud thud on the table. It was his payment from Berthold Oetker.

"Gold?" Craxi asked.

"Gold."

"Then I can have the weapon completed in three months."

"Good, by then I'll be the master of the Fortress at Metola, and you can move your work there. I'll provide you with as many assistants as you need."

"Excellent."

"One last thing, old man. Ideas come cheaper than most people imagine. I'm sure there are many military commanders walking the warfields of Europe pondering the future, speculating about the potential power of saltpetre. We need to move fast."

"I'm old, Malavolti; I *have* to move fast."

The dark knight was pleased, so he flattered the old man.

"I've been told by reliable sources that you're the greatest scientific genius in the Papal States."

"That's correct."

"I've also been told that having already achieved fame in your lifetime, you now crave everlasting immortality after the grave."

"You know many things about me that are exactly correct."

"Fine, then revolutionize the world with black-powder and make both of us rich."

"Is wealth all that you desire, young knight?"

"Yes," Malavolti replied without hesitation, as he walked to the door of the stone workhouse.

"I'll be back in two months, maybe three."

"I'll be ready," Craxi assured him.

Then the dark knight was gone, heading north with his cousin's putrid corpse to claim his inheritance.

Chapter 6

Parisio's Castle

Metola, the Papal States, September 1319

As the preliminary reading of the will droned on, Malavolti stood up from his isolated seat, turned his back to the dozen or so insignificants within the chamber, and stared out the window of the fortress. He was having trouble restraining his anger, restraining the impulse to unsheathe his sword and cut all of them down in their seats.

He tried to distract himself.

Parisio's castle was set on a high ridge in the rugged Apennine Mountains, and the dark knight was highly impressed with the sophistication of its defenses and its strategic location. The fortress was virtually impregnable, protected on three sides by precipitous slopes and guarded with a well-engineered moat and drawbridge, as well as sturdy walls and tower fortifications. It would be extremely hard, if not impossible, to siege the castle at Metola without the coming refinements of black-powder. Whatever his failings as a man, Parisio had been an intelligent warrior, and he'd clearly made significant improvements in the castle's defenses over the past few decades.

Down below, beneath a pure-blue Apennine sky, the castle's well-attended estates stretched into the valley towards the famed and valuable forests of Massa Trabaria. Malavolti estimated that well over a thousand peasants paid taxes and tribute to the wealthy castle at Metola, and the dark knight was determined, more than ever, to let nothing stand in the way of his claim to ownership, certainly not the preempting claims of two older Malavolti cousins whom he didn't even know existed until a few moments ago.

Word of Parisio's death had traveled fast, and one of his cousins had sent a judicial representative for the preliminary reading of the will. But it didn't matter who was actually present and who wasn't. The legal facts of the case were clear and simple: the dark knight was third in line to inherit Metola fortress. His initial impulse, when he learned about this unexpected and infuriating turn of events, was to hunt down the two cousins, murder them both, and seize the property.

In truth, Malavolti had no qualms about taking their lives. In the past, he'd never killed a man simply for wealth, but he'd also never felt as desperate before. Besides, he'd already slain hundreds of anonymous men on the battlefields of Europe. What were two more?

As the ecclesiastical lawyer continued his meticulous reading of Parisio's will, Malavolti realized that there might be another way.

A better way.

The bastard!

Although a bastard had no legal "right of claim," it could still inherit the estate if its father had chosen to make such a bequeathment. With little difficulty, Malavolti could arrange for a sophisticated forgery of a deathbed will in which Parisio would instruct that all his property should be turned over to his illegitimate child. Then Malavolti could track down the bastard and represent it himself. Eventually, when the time was right, when the property had legally passed into the bastard's hands, Malavolti would, through force or stealth, make it his own. Besides, the strength of his own sworn testimony would give enormous weight to Parisio's deathbed will, and Malavolti could also induce several prestigious perjurers to support his claim, including Berthold Oetker.

The entire deception could be effected in a matter of weeks if he could find the bastard quickly, and Malavolti was certain that he could find anyone he wanted to find. *Nothing* would stand in his way. At birth, he'd been deprived of a mother. At five, his father had been murdered in the Holy Land near Tripoli. At fifteen, his uncle and guardian, the great Templar Augustus Damiano, had perished fighting the Moors on the distant Iberian peninsula. Then, over the next two decades, his marriage had failed, and he was stripped of his birthright inheritance by the King of France, Philip the Fair. Malavolti had lost far too much throughout his difficult life to give up Metola without a fight.

For the dark knight, it would be a fight to the death.

Resolved, he turned back to the chamber and stared at the room of clerics, legal representatives, and clerks for the *Podesta* of Massa Trabaria. It was a room cluttered with pedants, dissimulators, calculators, and petty liars. He detested them all, and he was determined to undermine their efforts, to deceive the professional deceivers.

As the clerk continued with the will's listing of minor bequeath-ments, Malavolti looked away in disgust and stared into the waning fire of the chamber's largest fireplace. Within the flames, he conjured, as he often did, the fifty-four wooden stakes waiting on the outskirts of Paris beyond Porte Saint-Antoine.

It was nine years ago.

King Philip had exonerated Malavolti of his crimes against François Lucan, but the clever monarch had ordered the young knight into three years of exile. At the time, Malavolti had no personal wealth to support himself since his birthright, his father's financial legacy, had been tied up in the Templar's Bank in Paris, reputably the richest bank in the Europe. Thus Malavolti was forced by the treacherous king to spend his next three years as a "knight for hire."

A mercenary.

Then, as he was preparing to leave Paris, Malavolti heard the as-tonishing news that fifty-four members of the Temple had been con-demned to be burned to death by Philip's episcopal commission. He was stunned. Horrified. He knew full well the extent of the order's troubles, but he had no idea that it would come to this. No one did. It was perfectly clear that Philip would stop at nothing to seize the assets of the Templar vaults.

Three years earlier, in October 1307, the king had arrested every Templar in France, over five hundred monk-warriors, and through the machinations of his excommunicant chancellor, Guillaume de Nog-aret, he'd accused the order of apostasy, idolatry, treason in the Holy Land, and even sodomy. Every accusation was perfectly ludicrous, and no one knew it better than Malavolti. He might have lost his faith in the years since his uncle's death, but he'd lived amid the Templars during much of his youth at Acre, Cyprus, Ruad, and Paris, and he knew, without equivocation, that the charges against the Temple were totally false. At the time, he was convinced that, in spite of the political weaknesses of Pope Clement V, the case against the Templars would soon fall of its own weight.

Then, under torture, many of the Templars confessed, even the Grand Master Jacques de Molay, although most of them immediately recanted as soon as the threat of torture had passed. There are very few men in this world who can resist the pit, the rack, or the strappado, especially when combined with starvation and sleep-deprivation. During that period of time, when the papal commission was tediously investigating the false rumors about the order, Malavolti had been preoccupied with his own personal problems, which eventually lead to his exile.

But King Philip was extremely busy.

Fed up with the intractable papal investigation, the rapacious king took action himself. He appointed Philip de Marigny, the foppish brother of the Minister of Finance, as the Archbishop of Sens with authority extending over the bishopric of Paris. Then the king directed his new archbishop to immediately establish an independent episcopal commission to investigate the alleged crimes of the French Templars. The new commission convened on May 11th, and the very next day it condemned fifty-four Templars to "death at the stake" for refusing to confess to the fraudulent accusations.

Malavolti heard the stunning news just as he was about to leave Paris. In disbelief, he rode to Porte Saint-Antoine and watched in horror as fifty-four Templars, all wearing their red-cross white tunics, rode in a parade of wooden tumbrels that creaked eerily through the streets of Paris. Malavolti, of course, knew many of the Templars personally, and he'd always admired their boundless capacity for war, their piety, and their kindness. In his heart, the disgraced young knight wished that he could rise up with his sword, attack the imperial guard, and die defending the Templar brethren.

Instead, he did nothing but watch.

Stripped of their tunics, the Templars were bound to the stakes, each piled high with ready brushwood. Given a final chance to capitulate and confess, every single Templar knight refused. Then the merciful cry of "Strangulation!" rose up from the outraged crowd, but it went unheeded. It was a cry of sympathy since strangulation is clearly a far easier death than burning at the stake, but the king had already decided. One by one, the courageous Templars were set ablaze, and the people of Paris, who in the past had sometimes been jealous and suspicious of the Templars, were horrified by what they saw.

Malavolti, for the only time since he'd abandoned his faith, wished that he'd still possessed it. Like everyone else in the crowd, he wished that he could, in some small way, be like those courageous and saintly martyrs. When the carnage was over, he watched as the people of Paris sifted amid the ashes for relics of the Templar saints.

For about an hour or so, Malavolti watched the relic-hunters. Then, finally, he rode away from the city that had caused him so much pain. He was fully aware that Philip's actions against the Templars had been motivated by the king's desire for the wealth that supposedly lay hidden in their Parisian bank. He also knew that his birthright, as presently contained within the bank's frozen assets, was probably lost forever. But there was still a glimmer of hope. The Grand Master of the Temple was still alive, and the fate of Malavolti's legacy would inevitably rest on the final judgment of Jacques de Molay.

In the chamber at Metola, the scribe finally finished reading the will, and Malavolti stared over at everyone and spoke firmly.

With intimidation.

"This is all for nothing," he said dismissively, "and I demand a postponement."

No one responded.

They were all terrified by the huge powerful knight with the darkness in his eyes.

Malavolti continued:

"As you're fully aware, I was present at the deathbed of my cousin, Parisio, where I attended to his last wishes and witnessed his final will. It was made in sound mind, in good order, in the company of irreproachable witnesses. That legal document will be brought here to Metola in due time, in the proscribed manner. I stand here today, in the stead of my dead cousin, Parisio, to demand a hiatus of three months until his last and rightful will can be properly read."

The cowards in the room were both astonished and intrigued, especially in light of the fact that most of them had no real preference about whom the eventual heir might be.

Eventually, the presiding clerk addressed the dark knight.

"My lord, if you could indicate the principal beneficiary of that final will, it would help to expedite matters."

"The legal heir is a party unmentioned at today's proceedings, and I would like to assure you that the party under discussion is *not* myself. Nor have I ever met the individual."

This naturally created a great deal of interest and curiosity, as whispered discussions among those in the room emerged from the silence.

Malavolti cut them off.

"I have no time for prattle. I need to prepare the corpse of my cousin Parisio for burial, and I'd like a consensus on the postponement."

Malavolti glared down at the chief magistrate, and the man took the lead.

"Any objections?" he asked.

Only the legal representative of Parisio's cousin, raised his hand, but he said nothing.

"Noted," remarked the magistrate. "Then we'll meet here again in four months' time." Quickly, he checked the calendar on the table in front of him, "On January 6th."

"Good," Malavolti responded, as if to terminate any further discussion.

No one said a word.

As the clerk gathered his documents, the others drifted out of the chamber, and Malavolti, once again, turned away and stared out the window at the Apennine countryside.

The marvelously rich and lush estate stretched out before him. A man could live in great comfort here in Metola, with or without his proposed armaments income. Now all he had to do was find the Capitano's bastard.

Chapter 7

Santa Maria

Metola, the Papal States, September 1319

O utside the small stone chapel of Santa Maria, the dark knight dismounted and checked his peregrine. The bird was doing fine, fully accepting its various travels and the sudden loss of Lorenzo. Malavolti was pleased. In truth, the predatory falcon was the only thing that had given him any kind of recent satisfaction.

Unfortunately, his efforts at Metola castle to ascertain the identity of Parisio's bastard had borne no fruit, and the dark knight was frustrated and angry. Usually, Malavolti had no trouble gathering information, given that most people were intimidated by his presence, but he'd also learned over the years to recognize when people truly *didn't know* the information he wanted, and that was the case at Metola.

He'd been cautious and discrete, covering both the castle and the surrounding estates, talking to servants, officers of the garrison, and peasant farmers. No one had any awareness of the Capitano's "indiscretion," and most of them seemed astonished by the possibility, given

Lady Emilia's remarkable beauty and Parisio's well-known attentions to his wife. The only useful suggestion was that Malavolti should speak with Fra Cappellano at Santa Maria Chapel.

The dark knight tethered his black charger at the entrance and entered the stone mountain chapel. Inside, the little church was ordinary and empty, and the knight grew impatient. He was just about to call out when a young priest emerged from the sanctuary, knelt reverently on both knees before the altar, then walked back to the waiting knight. Although disappointed by the young man's age, he was pleased that he wasn't a Franciscan.

Malavolti wasted no time.

"How long have you served in this chapel?"

"Three months."

Oddly enough, the young cleric didn't seem frightened by the dark knight. He also had a humble serenity that particularly irritated Malavolti.

"And before you?"

"That priest is dead."

"Fra Cappellano?"

"Yes."

Malavolti was overcome with such a powerful frustration that it almost rose to the point of violence. He took a moment to control himself. These recent, reoccurring, almost irrational urges were not at all like the usually stoic Malavolti, but things had changed since that dark night in the garden near Niccone.

He did his best to push it from his mind.

When he'd regained his equilibrium, he continued.

"Who are you?"

"Ruffino. Fra Ruffino Ancona."

Malavolti nodded, attempting, without much success, to size up the young priest.

"I'm Parisio's cousin," Malavolti explained, "and I attended his deathbed. The Capitano wished to make amends to an injured party, and he told me to speak to Fra Cappellano about the family's secret."

"Well, I grew up in Metola, good knight, but I know nothing of Parisio's family secret."

"Nothing about a child?"

"Nothing," the young man responded, as if surprised by the question.

It seemed perfectly clear that the priest was telling the truth.

"Who *would* know?" Malavolti asked.

The young priest thought it over for a few moments. Then he glanced behind him at the left-side of the chapel.

"Look at this," he said.

Then the young priest led the towering black knight to a place near the front of the chapel where there was a dark recess within the stone wall at the level of the knight's knees. It was totally dark within the recess which seemed about a foot long and about a half-foot high. Curious, Malavolti bent down for a better look, and the priest removed a lit candle from a nearby rack.

"This might help," he suggested.

In the limited candlelight, Malavolti looked closer at the recess, and he was surprised to find that it was actually a hole through the wall. Then he reached up, took the priest's candle, and held it through the narrow aperture. Inside, there was a tiny, stone, windowless cell. It was dark, damp, and only a few feet high and a few feet deep. It reminded Malavolti of various torture chambers he'd seen in the underground vaults of certain castles in the Germanic states. Repulsed, he quickly withdrew the candle, handed it back to the priest, and stood up again.

"What is it?"

"A little home," the priest replied as he placed the candle back in the rack.

"*Nothing* could live in a hole like that."

"A pious dwarf lived inside that cell for thirteen years."

Malavolti, who had very few fears of earthly pain, felt a nauseating chill, and he didn't respond.

"The recess is situated here," the priest explained, "so that the poor creature could be close to the altar and participate in the Holy Sacrifice of the Mass. I'm told that the little dwarf received Holy Eucharist through that recess every single day for thirteen years."

The priest seemed delighted by the strange possibility.

Malavolti was revulsed.

"How did the little cretin eat?"

"Food was passed, once a day, through a second opening on the back wall of the cell. It can't be seen anymore because it's been sealed over."

Fed up, Malavolti returned to his original purpose.

"Why have you bored me with this unlikely story?"

"Because I was once told by Fra Cappellano, that the little creature knew *everything* about the house of Parisio."

"How was that possible?" Malavolti asked incredulously.

"I have no idea," the priest admitted.

"Where is it now?"

"I don't know that either, but I do know that it went to Mercatello during the Urbino invasion and never returned."

"When was that?"

The young priest thought it over.

"I was a boy at the time. It must have been about twelve or thirteen years ago."

It wasn't much to go on, but Malavolti had nothing else. Besides Mercatello wasn't that far from Metola, and he'd be foolish not to check it out.

Dissatisfied, but not completely discouraged, Malavolti took a gold coin from his belt and placed it in the priest's hand.

The cleric gave it back.

"It's not necessary," he said softly.

Insulted, Malavolti took the coin and tossed it disrespectfully toward the chapel's altar. Then he glared down at the young priest.

"Give it to the poor," he said.

With derision.

Then the dark knight left the stone chapel, mounted his charger, and prepared to ride to Mercatello. As he did so, he glanced up at the Castle of Metola. It was a truly magnificent sight, and he was determined to possess it for himself. Nothing would stop him. Not cousins. Not bastards. Not pious priests.

Certainly not dwarfs.

As he spurred his mount for Mercatello, he reassured himself.

"No matter what it takes, I'll find the little monster."

Chapter 8

Underground Chamber

Mercatello, the Papal States, September 1319

Malavolti followed the old crone down the stone steps into the damp darkness of the underground vaults. At first, they were somewhere beneath Parisio's Mercatello residence, but as they moved further into the darkness, through cold empty chambers and corridors, he felt that they were probably beneath the town's main palazzo.

The old woman moved slowly, carrying a lamp to light their way into the shadowed darkness. She was wary and silent, with a rosary around her neck. Malavolti knew that he'd have to tread softly with the old woman, known as Grisela, who'd once been an insignificant servant in Lady Emilia's service. He also knew that she couldn't be bribed or intimidated. He'd have to find another means of inspiring trust.

Finally, at the extremity of the underground vaults, the old woman stopped before a huge wooden door. Then she glanced at the dark knight, holding up the lamp close to the door's heavy bolts. Malavolti understood. Quickly, he undid the rusted bolts, opened the thick wooden door, and allowed the old woman to pass before him.

Inside, within a small freezing chamber, there was little to be seen. There was no real furniture, just a dilapidated wooden bench and an old wooden pallet. Everything stunk of sulfur and mold and dampness. Strangely enough, there was also nothing on the walls. No torch mounts. No lamp racks. Nothing to provide light within the dismal stone cell.

Several large rats suddenly scampered along the far wall then quickly disappeared into a crack in the masonry.

"The dwarf must have been pious indeed," Malavolti thought to himself, "to have endured an existence in this hellish darkness."

He turned to the old woman.

"Is this the place?"

The old woman nodded that it was. She seemed overcome with emotion, so Malavolti proceeded carefully.

"What else can you remember, Grisela?"

"I only saw the poor creature twice. Very briefly." She looked upward, into the dark eyes of the dark knight. "It was terribly hunchbacked, lame, and, I was told at the time, totally blind."

For the first time since the young priest at Metola had told Malavolti about the dwarf, he had a rush of pity for the afflicted creature. His own paternal grandmother had apparently gone blind in her later years, and although he'd never really known the woman, her condition had haunted him all his life. These days, when there was little sympathy of any kind remaining in the weary heart of the self-absorbed knight, he could still be moved by the thought of permanent blindness.

Eventually, however, he put his feelings aside and returned to the matter at hand.

"Was the dwarf a prisoner?"

"Yes," she remembered.

"For how long?"

"About a year."

But the memories were too much for the old woman to bear, so Grisela sat down on the old wooden bench and began to sob softly.

Malavolti said nothing.

He let her be.

He needed to be patient.

Eventually, he placed his hand gently on the old woman's shoulder and spoke with compassion.

"Trust me, Grisela, I've come to find the poor creature and make amends."

The old woman didn't respond.

"Trust me," he repeated. "It was Parisio's dying wish."

Exasperated, Grisela looked up with bewilderment in her eyes.

"How could Lady Emilia do such a thing to her own child?" she asked, not expecting an answer.

Malavolti was stunned.

Somehow, he managed to maintain a calm exterior, but within himself, he was amazed. The imprisoned dwarf had been Parisio's legitimate child! *Not* a bastard! Malavolti had never even considered such a possibility, but it would make his own objectives much easier.

It seemed that Lady Emilia had given birth to a deformed and sightless child. In shame, in guilt, both she and her husband had agreed to lock the pathetic creature away from the world and pretend that it didn't exist.

"I can't imagine," Malavolti responded, "but it's not my place to judge the dead. I'm here to rectify the present, to set things right, and I assure you that I will."

Since the old woman seemed convinced of the dark knight's good intentions, he proceeded.

"What happened to the child?"

"It disappeared. One day, my lord and my lady simply took the child away, and it never returned."

Frustrated, Malavolti asked the crucial question.

"Did it die?"

"No."

Once again, Malavolti flushed with hope, with a revitalized spirit.

"What happened, Grisela?"

The woman grew silent again, as Malavolti tried to contain his irritation. Nevertheless, his anger accelerated, and his patience evaporated, and he wondered if a knife at the old witch's throat might jar her memory.

It wasn't necessary. She decided to answer.

"I later heard rumors that the child was still alive."

"Tell me more."

"I know nothing more, young man, except the name of one of the soldiers who accompanied the family on that fateful journey."

"Tell me."

"Tebaldo Ugolino."

"Where is he?"

"Ravenna. In the service of the duke."

Malavolti's mind was racing, but he wasn't displeased. He could make it to Ravenna within three days, and the ancient city was full of excellent forgers. He could find Ugolino, have Parisio's final will drawn up, and even visit with his old friend Alighieri, the Florentine exile.

As he exited the chamber, the dark knight looked down at the old woman.

"You've done the right thing, Grisela."

He spoke with conviction.

"Please, my lord," she pleaded, "please help that poor creature!"

She grasped his hand.

"I will," he assured her.

"God bless you, young knight!"

Malavolti said nothing more.

Gently, he disengaged his hand and left the room for the corridors outside. He could find his own way through the darkness. The lurking rats, he smiled to himself, had better beware.

Chapter 9

Alighieri

Ravenna, October 1319

Malavolti read the final line of his friend's *Inferno* several times over:

And rose again to gaze upon the stars.

Very beautiful.

Then he thumbed back to Canto VIII to reread a short section in the fifth circle of hell. Throughout the manuscript, the narrator, Dante himself, follows his guide Vergil across the swampy Stygian lake that surrounds the infernal flaming city of Dis, the capital of hell. The boat, steered by Phlegyas, passes by many of the damned, who wallow up to their gagging throats in the slime and filthy mire. In their frenzied desperation, the doomed attempt to cling to the boat, trying to force their way onboard, when Dante suddenly recognizes, amid the muddy denizens of the hellish lake, the wealthy Florentine knight, Filippo Argenti of the Cavicciuli family:

> *And then I saw a vile muddy horde*
> *converge upon to maul the maddog knight,*
> *for which, in justice's sake, I praised the Lord.*

> *"Destroy Argenti!" the doomed cried in the night,*
> *whereas the Florentine turned upon himself*
> *and bit and tore his flesh with all his might.*

It was terrifying, and Malavolti was uncertain how to react. Filippo Argenti has been damned to the eternal mire for his transgressions of violence. For his wrathful temper. Uneasily, Malavolti admitted to himself that, over the past few weeks, he'd experienced a marked tendency in his own behavior towards inexplicable paroxysms of anger. An almost uncontrollable wrath. Naturally, he found such impulses disgraceful behavior for a confident and respected knight, and he had no idea how to deal with it, except as a matter of the will.

An assertion of his own free will.

Dissatisfied, Malavolti closed the *Inferno* manuscript and laid it down on a small table. Whatever he might think of the twin myths of hell and Christian redemption, there was no doubt that his friend Durante Alighieri, known as Dante, had written a sublime work of extraordinary power, scope, and depth. Malavolti could think of nothing comparable since Roman times, and he was proud, yet not surprised, at his friend's accomplishment.

Malavolti had enjoyed the first two days of his visit with Dante, and he'd made satisfactory arrangements with the master-forger Osimo. Now all he needed was the name of the dwarf, and that should be forthcoming since Dante's ancient servant, Luca, had gone to escort the Mercatellan soldier, Tebaldo Ugolino, to Malavolti for an interview. The dark knight, as was his nature these days, was still somewhat anxious, but after his recent discouragements, his overall plans were proceeding quite well.

Feeling a brisk rush of the coolish Adriatic air, Malavolti gazed outward, past the archbishop's Palace, towards the thick pine groves that Dante loved. The dark knight was sitting comfortably on the back verandah of Dante's villa in Ravenna, the ancient city where the Florentine exile had found protection under the generous patronage of Guido da Polenta, Lord of the City.

Ravenna, Malavolti reflected, was certainly a pleasant place to retire and compose one's poetry amid the countless ruins of the Caesars. Famous for its Byzantine mosaics – especially those at San Vitale, the Mausoleum of Galla Placidia, and Sant'Apollinare Nuovo – Ravenna had once been the ancient seat of both Roman emperors and barbarian kings, as well as the final outpost of the Byzantine empire. Malavolti could certainly appreciate why Dante was contented here, especially given the endless often-deadly chaos of his native Florence.

But it was there in Florence, over eighteen years ago, when a young, Assisi-born, French knight had met the great love poet and Florentine statesman while visiting on a diplomatic mission in the service of King Philip the Fair. In a flash of memories, Malavolti recalled the lively days of his youth and marveled at how much both he and Dante had changed over the years. Dante, in exile, had become the conscience of the Italian peninsula: a vocal proponent of unification as well as a fervent Christian demanding renewed spiritual rigor from the papacy. He was also, even before writing the *Commedia*, regarded as one of the most revered poets in Europe.

As for Malavolti, he preferred not to dwell on what he'd become: a mercenary warrior, who was nothing more than *just* a mercenary. He did wonder, nevertheless, how a man becomes what he becomes, thinking back to his youth in Paris. Remembering how he'd overcome the debilitating bitterness that overwhelmed him after the death in distant Iberia of his uncle, the mighty Templar Augustus Damiano, and how he soon succumbed to the high spirits of frivolous aristocratic life in Paris.

On the surface, it was an exhilarating time for a young, highly-skilled, secular knight who was uniquely attached to the king's elite cavalry as well as the Knights Templar. It was a time of high chivalry, of knighthood, of love poetry, of fashionable clothes, of scintillating balls at the royal palace. With romance. With captivating women. With lavish hunts. As well as gambling, dice, backgammon, chess, and even, on occasions, the latest Parisian fad, the racquet sport of tennis.

Malavolti had indulged himself in all these things with amused abandonment. To his great satisfaction, the Parisian ladies, despite the warnings of jealous noblesse, found his Italian coloring and his striking good looks irresistible. His well-known competence with the sword, his mysterious connections with the Temple, and his association with the unscrupulous Prince Rostand de Cornay further heightened the mystique of the young Assisian knight, and all of Paris seemed to be his for the asking.

Ask he did.

But now, sitting in Ravenna and looking back at his youth, Malavolti was fully aware how truly hollow and superficial everything had been. It was painfully embarrassing to recall the valuable time he'd wasted being clever for the ladies in the royal gardens and palace receptions, wearing foppish leather gloves, colored hose, and brightly embroidered tunics. In the end, it had brought him nothing of consequence, nothing but crushing heartbreak and endless dissatisfaction.

But before things had fallen apart, Malavolti had gone, in high spirits, to Florence with Prince Rostand to meet his favorite poet, the author of the Beatrice sonnets from *La Vita Nuova*. Alighieri, elected to the Priorate the year before, was one of the leading magistrates in Florence. He was thirty-six at the time, and although he'd certainly known both "women and wine" in his youth, he was now preoccupied with more serious matters, including the fate of the entire Italian peninsula.

The poet longed for a new empire, a new *Pax Romana*, and he detested French involvement on the peninsula. He particularly detested Philip the Fair and his shameless emissary Prince Rostand, although he still behaved civilly throughout the negotiations. He also took a special interest in the Italian-born Malavolti. So significant was the impact of Alighieri on the young knight that Malavolti had considered staying in Florence when the negotiations ended, but after the treaty was signed, he reconsidered and returned to his buoyant but trivial life in Paris.

The following year, when the French army of Charles de Valois installed the Black Guelph Corso Donati as the power in Florence, Dante was charged with a number of bogus crimes, and he ended up in permanent exile. Despite the poet's subsequent hardships, Malavolti always regretted his return to France with Rostand, wishing that he'd stayed in Florence and followed Dante into exile. Over the next few years, the two men corresponded sporadically, but, eventually, Malavolti, obsessed with other distractions in his life, cut things off.

As a result, he hadn't seen the great poet again until two mornings ago when he'd arrived in Ravenna. Nevertheless, he'd been greeted warmly, and Dante, who seldom hesitated to speak his mind, who'd always treated Malavolti like a younger brother, had, thus far, refrained from discussing the dark knight's many failings. Eventually, he would certainly have his say, and Malavolti was fully prepared to be patient.

Dante entered the verandah from the villa.

He'd aged, of course, but he still looked much the same: grave, pensive, medium build, with slightly stooped shoulders. His dark eyes were stern and deep-set in a longish Florentine face with distinctive brow and aquiline nose. It was said that Dante never forgot a slight and that he was humorless as well, but only the former was true. Almost fifty-five years old, Dante was still a zealot. Intense, passionate, and high-minded. But he could still smile and even poke fun at himself and the world around him.

"Did it put you to sleep?" he asked his guest.

"Not at all, Durante. Quite the contrary. It's truly extraordinary."

Malavolti hesitated, then decided to speak his mind.

"Would it flatter you too much, if I said that it stands with Aeneas?"

"At my age, Visco, it's impossible to be flattered too much."

The Florentine took a seat on the porch and stared off at the distant pines.

"I mean it," Malavolti assured him.

"I believe you, Visco. Whatever disagreements we might have had over the years, I've never known you to speak untruth."

This comment, carefully chosen by the poet, naturally upset Malavolti, but he maintained his silence. Was it true, he wondered, that even in his frivolous youth he'd been a more veracious man than the blatant deceiver he'd now become? Irritated by the thought, he pushed it from his mind and changed the subject.

"I'm delighted to see that Argenti wallows in the fifth circle."

Dante was surprised.

"Do you remember him?"

"Argenti introduced us eighteen years ago," the dark knight reminded the Florentine. "I remember him well. He was huge and powerful, but despicable and totally self-centered."

"Yes, he's hard to forget. He was a violently deranged knight, who was obsessed with wealth. Did you know that he was called Argenti because he shod his charger with silver?"

"No, I didn't, but I definitely remember that horse. It was magnificent."

Dante said nothing.

"But the man's temper was common," the dark knight remembered. "I once saw him beat his squire, and he was absolutely merciless."

"Yes, Filippo injured many people, which is why he's in hell."

"He certainly earned it," Malavolti said with a smile, but once again Dante didn't respond.

Then the dark knight recalled another telling scene in the *Inferno*:

"I also noticed that good King Philip is also confined to the lower regions."

"He earned it as well."

Malavolti nodded, and the poet changed the subject.

"I remember that you were once a talented poet yourself, Visco. Have you given it up?"

The dark knight shrugged.

"I suppose I've given up many things, Durante. Besides, I was only a fair talent."

"In my opinion, you had estimable talent."

Malavolti glanced down at the manuscript of the *Inferno* and responded, almost to himself.

"I could never have accomplished what you've accomplished. You've written about damnation with such depth and skill that even those of us who don't believe in hell can only marvel at what you've done."

"*Everyone* believes in hell."

When Malavolti didn't respond, Dante continued.

"*Everyone* believes that he'll be punished for his transgressions, even those who try to deny what they truly believe in their hearts."

Malavolti refused to argue. In truth, he didn't even want to think about it, but Dante wasn't finished.

"Unfortunately, too many of us will only admit to such a retribution after we've experienced hell on earth."

"I've seen that hell."

"You've seen nothing, Visco, but you will."

Malavolti attempted a laugh.

"Has the poet become a prophet in exile?"

"*All* poets are prophets, exiled or not," Dante said with a rare smile, "and I'm sure that you understand that I speak to you in the way that I do because I know you so well."

"Maybe it seems that way, Durante, but that was eighteen years ago, and I was only in Florence for three weeks. Much has changed since then."

Dante was undaunted.

"I know you so well, Visco, because we're so much alike." Then he added, as an afterthought, "Only our primary transgressions are different."

"What was *your* primary vice, Durante?"

The older man refused to avoid the question, growing grave, austere.

"I had *all* the ordinary sins, Visco, including the cheapest of all, common lust, but my foundational evil was philosophical transgression. A theological aberration. A self-satisfied denial of the truth."

Meaning a loss of faith.

The dark knight clearly understood Dante's meaning, and he had no interest in pursuing it any further.

"Now," Malavolti said with a forced smile, "I suppose you'll tell me *my* primary transgression?"

"No, my friend. You'll need to tell yourself."

The Florentine looked directly at Malavolti. Their eyes met. Briefly. Then Dante looked away, and the dark knight felt confident that their moral discussion was over. He was also pleased that his old friend had chosen not to say anything more than he had. Malavolti knew that the poet was well-intentioned, however foolish his religious convictions might be.

Dante rose up from his seat and pointed through the fading twilight at the archbishop's palace.

"Within that palace, Visco, is the chapel of St. Andrea, which has a rare, unique, and magnificent mosaic. Within this entire amazing city of spectacular mosaics, it's my personal favorite, and I'm not exactly sure why. It's a stunning portrayal of the haloed Christ as a warrior, wearing partial armor, crushing the heads of both a lion and a snake."

"You were once a warrior, Durante," Malavolti reminded the poet. "Didn't you ride with the front-line cavalry at Campaldino?"

"I did, and my ancestor Cacciaguida was knighted by Conrad III, and he was later killed by the infidels in the great disaster of the Second Crusade."

Malavolti had no idea that the poet was descended from a martyred Crusader.

"I've put him in *Paradiso*. It's my conviction that there are many more knights with God than there are with Satan."

They were both fully aware that Dante was really talking about Malavolti.

"Are my troubles so obvious?" the dark knight asked the poet.

"To me, they are, because, in *you*, my friend, I recognize myself from years ago." He looked down at Malavolti, "If I can help in any way, please let me know. Otherwise, I won't bring up the subject again, but you'll always be in my daily prayers."

Not certain what he should say, Malavolti simply nodded at his old friend.

"Now I see," the poet said, staring over the gardens, "that Luca is returning with your soldier."

Malavolti looked as well, seeing the two men who were walking down the garden path beside the villa.

"I'll see you at supper, my friend. Forgive me if I've offended you."

"You do it with concern," Malavolti responded, "with friendship. Which I understand."

Satisfied, Dante bowed to his guest and reentered his villa. As he did so, he waved at his servant, and Luca followed him inside.

Dante had conjured much in Malavolti's mind that the dark knight had no desire to contemplate, but he wasn't angry. He understood that Dante would always look upon him as a younger disciple, even a younger brother, and he didn't mind. The poet had sincere although misguided intentions.

Malavolti stood up to interrogate the Mercatellan.

The man who stood before him had obviously done a great deal of soldiering in his lifetime, maybe too much. He was somewhere in his mid-fifties, still solid, covered with battle scars that made him look even uglier than he was. It was obvious that the man was uncomfortable standing on the verandah of Dante Alighieri's villa, and Malavolti intentionally made him feel even more uncomfortable by staring at him, up and down, for a few moments in silence.

Finally, he addressed the man.

"I want information."

"Allow me to be of service, my lord."

"Are you a poor man, Ugolino?"

"I am."

Malavolti held up a sizable gold coin in the fading twilight.

"This is for you."

"Yes, my lord."

"I want to know about the deformed son of Parisio."

The soldier seemed astonished that anyone knew about the child, and he grew wary and hesitant.

Malavolti knew why.

"Are you aware that Parisio is dead?" he asked.

Ugolino shook his head to indicate that he didn't know, but he clearly believed Malavolti, and he was greatly relieved.

He looked at his inquisitor.

"It was a girl, good knight."

Malavolti was shocked.

Was it possible that such outrageous horrors had been inflicted on a helpless young girl?

"What was her name?"

"Margaret."

"Tell me what you know."

"After Parisio thwarted the Urbino invasion and secured a favorable treaty, he returned to a hero's welcome at his residence in Mercatello. Eventually, he and Lady Emilia planned to return to their castle in Metola. Around that time, several German monks came through the town telling amazing stories about miraculous cures that were taking place at the tomb of the recently dead lay Franciscan, Fra Giacomo di Castello.

"A few nights later, in total secrecy, I was part of a small detachment that accompanied Parisio, Lady Emilia, and a small, mysterious, veiled creature out of Mercatello. We headed south through the Apennines, over extremely rough roads, to Città di Castello.

"There were ten mounted men-at-arms in the escort, but we were told nothing. Nevertheless, on several occasions, I was required to carry the little creature, and I was astonished to realize that the little hunchback was a girl. Eventually, we took her into the cathedral that contained the tomb of Fra Giacomo. Then we were sent away.

"Later that night, we left the city from Porta Sant'Egidio with the Capitano and Lady Emilia, but without the little cripple. Under threat of death, we were ordered by Parisio to never discuss what had happened in Castello, but it was easy enough to figure it out."

"Tell me."

"The *Capitano* and his wife had taken the child to Castello, prayed for a miracle cure, and when it wasn't forthcoming, they abandoned the child."

Malavolti was amazed.

"Are you certain?"

"I am."

"Is the cripple still there?" Malavolti pressed, attempting to contain his excitement.

"Yes."

"Are you certain, soldier?" Malavolti asked with marked intimidation.

"I am, good knight. I've heard many rumors about the dwarf of Castello."

"Very good, take your coin and go."

Malavolti handed the gold piece to the grateful soldier, and the Mercatellan bowed deeply, then left immediately.

Satisfied in a manner that had evaded him for a long time, Malavolti stared out at the dark outlines of the city and the forests of Ravenna. It was very beautiful here, especially in the fast-fading twilight, but he couldn't have cared less. He'd already decided to forego his meal with Dante and leave the villa surreptitiously. He would take new lodgings at a local inn, and then, as soon as the forgery and the other legal documents were completed, he would leave Ravenna forever.

"Dante," he thought to himself, "can have his exile, his poems, and his self-righteous morality. Even his hells and his paradise! I'll take Metola!"

Chapter 10

Margaret

Città di Castello, the Papal States: October 1319

The dark knight, accompanied by his peregrine, rode through the rolling green hills of the upper Tiber Valley to the small market town of Castello. At the southern gate, under the cool gray skies of the late afternoon, he halted his charger above three beggar women.

"Do you know the dwarf named Margaret?"

"Everyone does, good knight," the eldest responded.

"Why is that?"

"Because she's a saint, my lord. A miracle-worker."

Malavolti nearly laughed out loud.

"Do you know where she is?" he asked.

"She stays at the palace of Lord Venturino."

Malavolti didn't bother to comment on the unlikelihood of a saint living in a palace. The little creature was probably some kind of curiosity for the local baron. Regardless, Malavolti was satisfied, and he tossed a few coins to the fawning beggars.

"God bless you, good knight," they called after him.

Malavolti said nothing, then rode away. In truth, he was weary of hearing that meaningless rote expression, "God bless you," so he ignored it. Instead, he headed towards the high campanile adjacent to the city's main cathedral near the central piazza.

He wondered if it was the same cathedral where Parisio and his wife had abandoned their deformed child, but it really didn't matter. The dark knight reminded himself that Margaret would no longer be a child. From everything he'd learned over the past few weeks, he estimated that she'd now be in her late twenties, if not early thirties. But, of course, that also didn't matter.

In the center of city's busy piazza, Malavolti questioned a young fop about the location of Venturino Palace. Glad to be of assistance, the young man pointed at the higher part of the city.

"Just beyond that tower," he explained, "there's an impressive residence that's soft blue in color. Lord Venturino lives there with his wife."

Malavolti nodded and continued his way through the city. Everything was going well. As well as he could have wished. If the little dwarf had turned to religion to help her deal with her deformities, then all the better. A saint would certainly have no need for a castle. As for Venturino, whoever he might be, Malavolti had no concern about any kind of interference. He was too closely allied with the mercenary warlord Berthold Oetker for some petty local noble to dare intrude on his plans. The very mention of the name Oetker would make this little trading town tremble at its foundations.

Malavolti was gratified.

He was confident.

In Ravenna, Osimo had done a masterful job on Parisio's last will, and before the dark knight had left the ancient city, he'd hired a number of high-priced lawyers to manufacture a legal document that would transfer, after a period of two months, the entire Metolan inheritance of Margaret of Castello to Visconte Malavolti, knight-at-arms. All he needed now was the signature of some pathetic female dwarf, and the castle of Metola was his forever, and absolutely nothing in this quiet little town, he was certain, would stand in his way.

As Malavolti passed the northern tower, the bells of the adjacent church began to ring. Loudly. Without cessation. In time, the other churches of the city, including the cathedral, were sounding their huge church bells into the cooling twilight. Soon the streets were filled with workmen, who'd obviously dropped everything they were doing, and were now running through the streets before the dark mounted stranger. Malavolti, of course, knew exactly what it meant, but he paid no attention, feeling no inclination to help.

On cool evenings like tonight, it was not uncommon for families to let their fireplaces burn too high, and, not infrequently, an unseen spark would fly out of a raging hearth and ignite the house itself. In a crowded town like Castello, with its many winding narrow streets and its countless wooden balconies, the danger of a rapidly spreading conflagration was especially concerning. If the Castellans weren't careful, their entire town could go up in flames. Which was fine with Malavolti, as long as he got his signature.

As he continued on his way through the increasing commotion of the fire brigades, something shuddered hard within the dark knight.

It jarred his entire being. He could sense some kind of danger, and he had the unfailing premonition that the fire was emanating from the Venturino residence. Panic-struck, Malavolti spurred his mount forward and rode recklessly though the crowded streets toward the rising flames.

When he arrived at the scene of the fire, it was, as he expected, a small yet attractive palace, light blue in color. From its rooftop, Malavolti could see the ravenous flames as dark black smoke filled the early evening sky. Milling around the residence, there was a large anxious crowd in obvious disarray, even though the two bucket chains seemed to be working with efficiency, passing wooden buckets through the front entrance into the palace. Malavolti, of course, had seen hundreds of fires in his lifetime, and he'd set many himself. At a single glance, he knew that the palace was lost.

Furious, he rode his mount to the front door of the building. Standing next to the senior fire warden, there was a rather dignified well-dressed woman whom Malavolti assumed was Lady Venturino. The woman stared up at the flames with horror, with an agonizing helplessness. Before Malavolti had a chance to speak, she turned to the warden.

"Can nothing more be done?"

The old man refused to deceive.

"I'm afraid not, my lady. I'm afraid your home is lost."

Then the woman, with remarkable courage, nodded with acquiescence.

The dark knight intruded.

"Where is Margaret of Castello?" he called down from his charger.

Confused, Lady Venturino glanced up at Malavolti, then turned to a sobbing housemaid.

"Isn't Margaret at the prison?"

"No, my lady," the young girl sobbed, "she's up in her garret praying her office."

Malavolti looked at the top of the building.

If the stupid dwarf was still alive in that smoking garret, he'd track her down, retrieve her, and carry her back down to the street.

As Malavolti dismounted, Lady Venturino rushed into the entrance of her home, and the dark knight followed into the burning building. Inside, the palace was a raging inferno, thick with smoke, heavy with a throbbing yet invisible wall of singeing heat. At the bottom of the stairs, the leading three members of the fire brigade had dropped their useless water buckets and were now attempting to restrain Lady Venturino.

"Margaret!" she called out in desperation. "Margaret! Come down!"

Malavolti paid little attention to the commotion. Quickly, he looked around. Embers from the main fireplace on the ground floor had apparently ignited the right-side wall, and the fire had climbed upstairs where it was burning with frenzied ferocity. Even the stairs were partly consumed.

Malavolti was undaunted. He was fully determined to ascend to the second story. The dark knight had been burned before, in various military conflicts, and he'd always found it the most horrible of injuries, but nothing would stop him now. Instantly, he undid his sword, dropped it to the floor, and rushed to the base of the stairs.

"Margaret!" Lady Venturino continued to cry out.

Hopelessly.

Suddenly, oddly, as Malavolti began to mount the burning staircase, everything inside the palace, except for the malicious crackling of the flames, grew preternaturally still. Stopping where he was on the stairs, the knight looked down at Lady Venturino and the others around her. Then, seeing where their attentions were focused, he followed their gaze to the second-floor landing.

On the interior balcony, within the strangely glowing orange lights of the leaping flames, the dark knight saw an eerie figure emerge from the smoke. Then it stared down through the second-story railing. Its face was disproportionate in every way, and yet it was not totally displeasing. Seeming more bizarre than ugly. The face was lit by another kind of fire, an abnormal almost unearthly serenity.

Which frightened Malavolti.

Calmly, the little creature pressed its peculiar face forward to look down at her terrified friend, Lady Venturino.

"Be calm, dear Griga," she said with a smile. "Don't be afraid. Have confidence in God."

Lady Venturino, although relieved to see that her little friend was still alive, was naturally terrified to see Margaret completely surrounded by the swirling flames. The dwarf, apprehending the depths of her friend's fears, began to move mysteriously within the unclear haze of the smoke and fire. Then Malavolti realized that she was simply taking off her small black cloak. When she was done, she tossed it down to her friend.

"Cast it into the fire."

Given the circumstances, Malavolti felt certain that he'd never heard anything so ridiculous in his entire life, but, for some reason, he stayed right where he was and watched as Lady Venturino picked up the small black cloak and hurled it, as well as she could, over the rabid flames that were furiously leaping into the room from the right-side wall. Suddenly, inexplicably, the flames withdrew from the little cloak, subsided, then vanished altogether. Nothing was left but ash, smoke, and diminishing heat.

With the exception of Lady Venturino, everyone in the room was stunned in a disbelieving silence, and no one was more incredulous than Malavolti. He'd clearly seen what he couldn't believe, and he was infuriated by the obvious disorder of his faculties. Furious, he kicked at the smoldering steps, then he glanced up at the second floor again.

The lingering smoke was still obscuring the landing, but the fire was gone.

Completely.

Then he saw it again.

The strange face of the dwarf emerging from the haze and gazing directly at him. Gazing directly into his eyes. It seemed expressionless, but it wasn't, and it was terrifying. It was an uncanny mixture of too many things at once: disorder, concern, serenity, even some kind of personal challenge. The dark knight was astonished to find himself flush with fear, something that he'd seldom experienced in his entire life, certainly not from the single look of another human being.

Then the face was gone.

Confused, exasperated, choking in the billowing smoke, Malavolti backed down the staircase, exited the building, and stepped outside into the cool Castellan night.

Chapter 11

Precipice

Città di Castello, the Papal States: October 1319

H e stood at the edge of the precipice and stared down into the darkness.

Above him, there was a slight distant moon and a few faint stars in the cold night sky. Neither did anything to lighten the blackness that lay beneath him, which seemed close and depthless. For the past few hours, the weary knight had felt powerfully compelled to leap to his death, not just to end his present torment, but to violently bash himself open on the unseen rocks below.

Something foul, something incomprehensible, had overcome him tonight, and he felt as though he was in the throes of some kind of madness, some kind of delirium, yet he still seemed to have all of his faculties, including his reason, which, it seems, had rebelled against him, torturing him to distraction.

With all his willpower, the warrior knight tried to resist his deranged impulses, trying to distract himself, but no matter how hard he tried, the same recurring images flashed before him: the slaughter of the Christians in Acre, the news of his uncle's death, the burning of the Templar knights, the vitriolic condescension of François Lucan, the death of Jacques de Molay, the horrible night with Zampa in Niccone, and the monstrous freakish face of the malicious dwarf.

Of all these things, the most dreadful was the face of the hunchback.

Or maybe that terrible night in Niccone.

Or maybe the execution of Jacques de Molay.

All of which continually flashed through his disordered mind.

Over and over again.

Then it was Molay again.

Five years ago.

Malavolti's final day in Paris.

His exile had been over for several months, and his fortune had already been sealed by the papacy's dissolution of the Templars two years earlier, as well as the subsequent seizing of the Temple bank by Philip the Fair. Nevertheless, as long as the Grand Master, whom Malavolti had known and admired throughout his life, was still alive, maybe there was still a faint reason to hope.

Maybe there was still a final shred of hope remaining within this vile and accursed world.

On March 18, 1314, Jacques de Molay, in heavy chains, stood on a huge wooden platform that had been constructed outside Notre Dame, in front of a grandstand of nobles and ecclesiastics and a huge mob of Parisian onlookers. Defiantly, the embattled knight reasserted his innocence and that of the order he'd served his entire adult life.

Malavolti stood there that day watching, and he remembered everything, remembering exactly what the great Templar had said:

> *Before heaven and earth, and with all of you for my witnesses, I confess. I confess that I am indeed guilty of the greatest infamy. But that infamy is that I have lied. I have lied in admitting the foul disgusting charges laid against my Order, and I declare – I must declare – that the Order is totally innocent. Its purity and saintliness have never been defiled. In truth, although I have testified otherwise, I did so only from fear of the most horrible tortures.*

The next day, the king's elite guard rowed Jacques de Molay and Geoffrey de Charney, the Templar Preceptor of Normandy, to Île aux Javiaux, a small island in the middle of the Seine River. Even with the formidable armed might of the House of Capet at his disposal, Philip the Fair still feared burning the two distinguished men in the streets of Paris. So they were taken to Île aux Javiaux, and Malavolti, aware of what was happening, bribed a local boatman to take him to the island as well.

Once there, the two Templars were again given the opportunity to recant and save their lives, but they both refused. They only asked for God's forgiveness. They were then stripped of their red-cross tunics, bound to stakes, and set to flame. Malavolti watched the nightmare from beginning to end, and he did nothing. It wasn't cowardice or even the fear of death that stayed his hand. In truth, by then, Malavolti was fully prepared for death.

He took no action that terrible day because he felt overwhelmed with hopelessness. With bitter incomprehensible despair. Which immobilized his mind and paralyzed his spirit. If the mighty Templars, who'd willingly shed their blood for Christ and the faith in the Holy Land, could be castigated as evil and exterminated from the face of the earth, then earth itself was nothing but desolation.

Nothing but waste.

Worse than the myth of hell.

Later that night, the pious Christians of Paris swam through the Seine to Île aux Javiaux and searched for relics amid the ashes. Eventually, as they swam back home, they carried the holy shards of the saints, still warm from the fire, safely in their mouths. But Malavolti was certain that he could never salvage anything from the ruins, so he took his boat back to the city and left Paris the same night, fully expecting, fully hoping, to die on the distant battlefields of Scotland.

Then it was the dwarf again.

Once again, he conjured the terrible gaze of the deformed dwarf within the darkness before him. His eyes were enflamed with the sight, as if painfully singed. He could clearly see the little witch exactly as she was, no longer bathed in the mysterious lights of the swirling fires, but in the undeniable reality of her unearthly ugliness.

Yes, the dwarf was disfigured and lame and hunchbacked, but its truest deformity was its disproportionate head and face: its glazed and sightless eyes, its overly-broad forehead, its narrow tapered chin, its small teeth, its projecting nose. *Nothing* was appropriate. *Nothing* was right. Nothing fit together, as Malavolti tried, without effect, to shake it from his mind.

Earlier this evening, when her terrible visage had vanished back into the smoke in Venturino's palace, Malavolti, in a kind of stupor, had staggered out of the smoldering house, parting the crowd before him. Then he wandered alone for hours throughout the dark city. Inexplicably, he'd left behind his sword, his mount, his peregrine, and his legal documents. He was fully aware that his behavior was totally irrational, but he never went back.

Racked with revulsion, with a kind of deadly anxiety, he stopped at a small tavern to try and drink his terrors away, but he gagged on the wine and left. Later, walking the streets again, he approached a common whore, something he'd never done in his entire life. But when he stared into the woman's lifeless eyes, he was horrified, and he walked away. Finally, repulsed by everything, by himself, by other people, even by the city itself, he unthinkingly wandered into the countryside, into the surrounding hills.

For hours, Malavolti roamed about, lost, without direction, until he'd ended up right here, high above the darkness, far from the distant dimly-lit city. He had no idea what he was doing. Or why. But he was convinced that the ugly dwarf had bewitched him in some way. Maybe cast a spell of some kind. Which was hard for Malavolti to admit, even in his present derangement, because he didn't believe in such things. He was a highly-educated and rational man, not some stupid superstitious peasant. He didn't believe in spells, or curses, or enchantments, or miracles.

In truth, he didn't believe in anything.

At the age of fifteen, he'd willfully abandoned everything that he'd previously believed when he learned that his uncle Augustus had died in some godforsaken battle in southern Iberia. For what? Everyone assured him that his uncle had died a warrior and a saint, but Malavolti didn't care. All he knew was that his uncle was dead and that his own life was suddenly empty, bitter, and godless.

Only the tantalizing lures of Parisian pleasures and easy companionship had lifted him out of his despondency at the time. But eventually those superficialities failed him as well. Soon he was entirely alone, this time in exile, with only a threatened financial inheritance to look forward to, until the malicious prosecution of the Temple put an end to that. Beginning with the day he was born, when his mother had died, Malavolti had been continually deprived of everything that he'd ever valued in this useless and pathetic life, and he'd ended in a perpetual state of profound and depthless mistrust.

It was the kind of hopelessness that went far deeper than simple atheism because it was an atheism of everything, not just the myth of god, but of his entire supposed creation. It wasn't anxiety. Or doubt. Or fear. Malavolti never gave quarter to such failures of the will. No, it was a willful consent to the utter futility and ineffectuality of everything that existed in the world around him.

It was, in effect, an assent of utter hopelessness, and until tonight, Malavolti had always been strong enough to both accept it and live through it. But the mesmerizing face of the bizarre Castellan dwarf and her magic within the flames had, for some inexplicable reason, forced Malavolti to fully confront what he really was. What he'd *really* become.

Which was more terrifying than he could bear.

Standing alone in the darkness, Malavolti realized that he had only two desires left in this life: to decapitate the monster-dwarf and to bash his own existence into nothingness. For some reason, he believed that the first was impossible, whereas the second was not only possible, it was looming right in front of him.

Beckoning.

Malavolti stared down into the gulf of the blackness that lay beneath him, and he experienced a sudden and comforting vertigo. He recollected the words of Dante:

> *Their cries and groans and desperate lamentation*
> *Smote uselessly against the starless night.*

With condescension, even with hatred, Malavolti damned Dante and his absurdist little hells.

Then he succumbed.

He leaned himself outward into the darkness, slipped, and fell forward, anticipating the freefall rush of an instant descent to his death on the rocks below. It never came. Instead, he thumped down to a sitting position on a narrow stone ledge beneath the edge of the cliff, where his weight and its impact had dislodged much of the stone shelf. The dark knight twisted in the darkness, hanging helplessly, as he started sliding off the side of the precipice.

His mind was now consumed with nothingness.

A nothingness that was dark and deadly, yet attractive and welcome. Nevertheless, for some inexplicable reason, neither fear nor self-preservation, he reached up with his right hand, grabbed the stone edge of the cliff, and dangled precariously. Numbed, essentially mindless, he considered releasing his grip, then he decided to do so. But he didn't. For some unfathomable reason, he reached up his left hand, gripped the edge, and despite the difficulties and the crumbling rocks, he pulled himself back up, then over the edge, lying exhausted on top of the cliff.

He didn't know why.

Desperate, he turned over on his back, and he stared into the dark skies above him, remembering everything he was capable of remembering about the terrible night that he'd killed his squire and killed the Franciscan.

He hated the sky.

He hated the pale stars.

He hated himself.

He hated everything, everywhere, and he hated it for the simple pleasure of hatred itself. There was nothing left for Malavolti in this useless world, and now he seemed incapable of ending his own life.

But there was something else.

Something truly terrifying.

The absolute certainty that he wasn't alone.

Chapter 12

Prison

Città di Castello, the Papal States: October 1319

The next morning, having retrieved his sword, his charger, and his falcon, Malavolti glared down a guard at Torre Civico, the city's ancient fortress tower, dismounted his horse and stormed, unescorted, into the Castellan prison. He looked dangerous. He looked violent. He was wide-eyed and seemingly disturbed. Somehow, he'd managed to survive his night of darkness on the Castellan cliffs, but the very same agonies were still racking within his mind and his soul, and he was determined to do something about it.

Impervious to the sufferings around him, the dark knight moved quickly from chamber to chamber through the cold dark prison which reeked of disease, dampness, and mold. He paid no attention to the pathetic prisoners, chained to the stone walls, who were either howling in despair or dying silently on their wooden pallets. He hardly noticed them. He had only one obsessive preoccupation.

Finally, he found the little creature in a large underground chamber which served, inadequately, as the prison's infirmary. Several hopelessly diseased men were lying on makeshift beds, attended by three Mantellatas, known as the Veiled Ones, including the blind little hunchback who was leaning on a small wooden crutch. Malavolti strode to the center of the room, and everyone, stunned by his formidable aspect, looked up in fear. Except for the Mantellata dwarf, who turned around and gazed her blind, glazed, lightless eyes in the dark knight's direction.

She was apparently a Dominican tertiary of some kind, a lay member of the Order of Penance. She was dressed, like the other sisters, in a white tunic with a leather belt, with a soft white veil, with the distinctive black cloak known as the mantella. Malavolti, despite his irritation at the distraction, briefly wondered if it was the same cloak that had miraculously extinguished the fire at Venturino's palace.

He felt certain that it was.

Furious, yet unsure why, the dark knight stared down at the miserable little creature who calmly confronted him.

"You're a monster!" he said.

With revulsion.

She replied gently.

With conviction.

"I'm a child of God."

"God is nothing but a monster himself."

"God is the Father who loves His children. *All* of them."

Malavolti drew his sword. He would put an end to this nonsense right now. Off to his left, one of the other Mantellatas gasped in horror, but little Margaret, clearly aware of what he was doing despite her blindness, stared at Malavolti with the one particular look that the dark knight couldn't tolerate.

A look of compassion.

He raised his sword.

"No!" cried one of the other tertiaries.

But Margaret was eerily calm and unintimidated. She folded her hands together and looked directly into the blasphemer's eyes.

"I'm always ready to join my God, my Father."

Then little Margaret seemed to withdraw into herself, and Malavolti knew exactly what she was doing. She was praying, and she wasn't praying for herself, she was praying for *him*. He was absolutely certain about it, and he was enraged by her presumption. It was time to put an end to this farce.

The dark knight tightened the grip on his upraised sword.

Then, as he was about to slash down his weapon and bisect the little cretin, he glanced, once more, at her face. But now it was no longer the frightening visage that had tormented him last night in the darkness at the precipice. It was still, to be sure, a disordered and disproportional visage, but it was also gentle, inexplicably serene, and oddly not unpleasant. Her face, lost as it was in prayer, seemed to luminate with a pacificity that was akin to a kind of beauty.

Which further enflamed his anger.

His humiliation.

Raising his left hand to the hilt of his sword, Malavolti slashed the weapon downward with a furious rush of the prison's stagnant air. Behind him, one of the Mantellatas cried out, as his sword, an exact duplicate of his uncle's Templar sword, flashed in front of the face of the little tertiary and sunk into the dark dirt floor of the prison.

Astonished, overcome by his incomprehensible cowardice, Malavolti fell to his knees to curse the accursed God that he'd sensed, all last night, watching him in the darkness on the precipice. In agony, the dark knight dropped his head to his chest and, with all of his strength of will, refused to acknowledge the ever-present intolerable God in any way, except as the object of his hatred.

It passed.

Gradually.

But not his confusion, and not his terror, but rather the force of his violence. He was completely worn down. Worn out.

He'd expended himself.

Then the room grew unnaturally still, and he sensed a glow of heat within the chilly chamber. Even though it seemed impossible, he recognized the scent of roses. He lifted his head and stared at the little Mantellata, who now hovered slightly above him. In the heat of her ecstasy, the little tertiary had somehow risen from the dirt floor of the prison and was now hovering in the air in front of him. Disbelieving his senses, Malavolti tried to reorder his mind, but there was no doubt. Margaret had elevated, or somehow levitated, over four feet into the air. She seemed oblivious to everything around her, as if temporarily lost in some kind of transformative meditative state.

Stunned, Malavolti, who'd always scoffed at the miraculous, stared intently at the pious woman's transported face until it became unbearable.

He lowered his head.

He hadn't succumbed to anything, and he certainly hadn't attempted to pray, but for some reason, the malicious bitterness that had racked his spirit for nearly thirteen hours had dissipated. But he was still wary. He had no confidence that the current break in his torment was permanent, even though he was grateful for a few brief moments of inexplicable peace.

Finally, when he looked up again, Margaret was no longer in front of him. No longer elevated. Then he felt her gentle hand touching his shoulder.

He heard her voice.

"Be patient, dark knight, you've survived a most difficult night. A night of despair."

Malavolti, still on his knees, turned to face her.

He wanted her to stay.

He wanted to talk.

"Don't go."

"I must," she said softly, "but I'll be back tonight."

Malavolti nodded, and the woman's little hand rose from his shoulder. Then, from behind, he could hear the uneven alternating sounds of her lame steps and her wooden crutch as she was guided from the chamber by her sister Mantellatas.

Chapter 13

Alonzo di San Mario

Città di Castello, the Papal States: October 1319

Malavolti spent the entire day and the entire evening bathing incapacitated prisoners, cleansing their foul ulcers, bandaging their wounds. He felt it was a woman's work, or a medic's at best, but the dark knight did it anyway. He kept himself occupied, saying nothing all day long, trying to keep his mind a blank until the little dwarf returned. In the meantime, her sister Mantellatas, respectfully, gently, directed his work. Despite what had happened this morning, the criminals also addressed him with honor, referring to Malavolti as "my lord" or the "dark knight," sometimes recollecting for their unlikely benefactor amazing stories about the "little saint."

During the course of his long day, Malavolti was informed by various brigands, murderers, and political prisoners that the deformed nun often levitated during her prayers, especially during her stays at the prison. Amid the squalor. Amid the suffering. The other nuns had done their best to kept it a secret in an effort to avoid curiosity seekers, but, apparently, Margaret had plenty of that anyway, given her reputation as a miracle-worker in Castello. By all accounts, she managed it well, with understanding, with compassion.

Most of Margaret's time, when she wasn't praying, was spent providing food to the poor and care for the dying and imprisoned. She was reputed to be kind to everyone, regardless of their station in Castellan society, and she was much loved by the citizens of the city. Even certain jealousies about her miraculous spirituality had, in time, resolved into reconciliations, if not outright discipleships. It seemed that everyone, when the little saint wasn't around, liked nothing more than discussing her many marvels and miracles.

She'd also, apparently, made a number of startling prophesies about various people in Castello which had all come true, amazing everyone in the city. One that stood out in Malavolti's mind was her improbable prediction that a worldly and wealthy noble's wife, Lady Ysachina Macreti, who'd adamantly refused to allow her daughter to become a Mantellata, would herself become a Dominican tertiary. Like everyone else in the city, Ysachina laughed it off with nothing but condescension, but a few months later, after her husband died unexpectedly, she experienced a profound religious conversion, and, along with her daughter, took up the black mantella.

There were also countless miracles: knowing significant facts about people whom she'd never met, knowing word-for-word the texts of rare theological tracts, healing the infirmaries of various strangers, curing her dying goddaughter, and, of course, her most recent miracle, extinguishing the out-of-control fire at Venturino Palace. All day long, as he went about his chores, Malavolti listened to the many stories, but he said nothing. He had neither the will nor the desire to question such things right now. Besides, he'd already seen too much that was totally inexplicable. So he went about his work, comforting the suffering, as he waited for Margaret's return, never once thinking about the castle at Metola.

He did, however, think a great deal about little Margaret, and he grew quite concerned when the eight o'clock hour had passed, and she hadn't returned. His anxiety was not only for himself. He was specifically concerned for the dying emaciate man who lay before him on one of the wooden pallets.

Malavolti had seen as much death as any man, and he knew, without doubt, that this feverish incapacitate man would soon be dead. He also knew that the man, whenever he was briefly conscious, would ask for "little Margaret," wondering when she'd return. When Malavolti had finished his chores for the day, he sat with the wasted man, who was about his own age, and watched his struggles. Suddenly, unexpectedly, the feverish man opened his eyes, regained lucidity, and stared at Malavolti with a peculiar smile.

"So you're the blaspheming knight?" he said, almost with amusement.

The dark knight made no response.

"Do you know who I am?" the dying man asked.

Malavolti had no idea.

"Alonzo di San Mario," the skeletal man said, but the man's name meant nothing to Malavolti.

"I was once worse than you," Alonzo remembered. "I was the blasphemer of all blasphemers, and I felt that I had good reason."

"What was that?"

"The injustice of everything in my entire life," the man recalled, then explained. "My foolish brother had gotten himself involved in some kind of political intrigue, so his enemies seized me, tortured me close to death, then threw me into this terrible dungeon.

"As I lay here in chains, helpless and crippled, my wife and young son fell into destitution. Unable to help them, I went insane with anger, and I blamed God even more than my tormentors. Eventually, I learned that my little boy died of starvation last winter, and for many months, I lay in this foul place and cursed God, and all the good sisters, and little Margaret most of all."

He paused, recollected his thoughts, and continued.

"Finally, one day, when the time was right, Margaret came to my side, and she gave me hope. She offered me comfort and peace."

Alonzo stared at Malavolti.

"Later tonight, I'll be escaping this vile place, and I'll meet again with my son."

"Do you really believe that?"

"I do. I have no doubt."

Malavolti said nothing, so the man continued.

"Men like us need to learn to trust."

"Trust what?"

"Trust in anything but yourself," the man explained. "At least, for now."

Again, the dark knight said nothing, as the afflicted man seemed to drift away into unconsciousness.

"I thirst," he whispered.

Malavolti lifted a cup of water, but it was useless. The man's delirium had returned. Malavolti dipped his finger into the water then wiped it gently across the man's parched lips.

It was futile, but he did it again.

Then he heard her footsteps.

He heard the soft thump of the crutch in the dirt. He turned around as Margaret entered the infirmary with another tertiary and an elderly Dominican friar. The dark knight immediately stood up and backed away from Alonzo's deathbed, as Margaret, guided to the bed by her sister Mantellata, took Alonzo's hand and gently roused him back to a semi-coherent consciousness. Instantly, the friar knelt down, heard the man's final confession, and administered last rites.

When the priest was done, he stood up, gently tapped Margaret on the shoulder, and left the room escorted by the other tertiary. Then, for almost an hour, the deformed little nun and Alonzo di San Mario softly whispered to each other like dear old friends until the man finally lapsed into sleep. He died about an hour later. He turned his head, coughed some blood on his chest, then shuddered lightly before he was gone. It wasn't a pleasant sight, and it certainly wasn't miraculous, but Malavolti still wished that the spirit of the dead man might somehow, somewhere, be reunited with the son he'd loved so much.

"Do you believe he's in heaven?" the dark knight asked the little tertiary.

"He's not in hell," she replied gently.

Then she turned to face the man who'd, earlier this morning, tried to kill her.

"Come closer," she said softly.

Malavolti stepped forward. Then he sat down in an old wooden chair beside the pallet, in front of the little nun.

"I often find myself," she said, "thinking of St. Joseph. Especially his trials leading the Child and the Virgin into Egypt."

It seemed an odd thing to be thinking about.

"Have you ever considered the situation?" she asked Malavolti, not really expecting an answer. "All the armies of Herod the Great were seeking to slaughter the little Child, the child begotten of the Holy Spirit, the child who would call St. Joseph his father. Then, on the strength of an angelic dream, Joseph rose up immediately and surreptitiously led his young wife and her newborn Infant on the difficult journey south across the desert into an alien and hostile land. Yet he succeeded. He overcame both the elements and the terrain, and he dodged Herod's troops, and he cared for his Madonna and Child."

When she finished her seemingly-random thoughts, Malavolti thought it over carefully. In his youth, he'd read about the Flight into Exile many times, but he'd never given it much thought.

"Joseph put his trust in God," the Mantellata said softly. "It's what we all need to do."

Malavolti nodded.

He understood.

For some reason, he didn't mind the little tertiary speaking to him as she had. He accepted it. Then he glanced down at the dead Alonzo, and he remembered what the suffering man had said earlier about trust. Malavolti certainly wasn't ready to trust in some kind of irrational concept like "God," but he could, for the time being, do as so many others had done, trust in this strangely deformed and comforting nun.

He looked back at Margaret, staring into her sightless eyes.

"Do you know why I came to Castello?"

"Yes."

"How could you know such a thing?"

She shrugged.

"I have no idea how I know some of the things I seem to know. I'm simply a vessel that, sometimes, inexplicably, knows things. There's no explaining it. There's no understanding it."

Although he wasn't fully satisfied with her answer, the dark knight could see that Margaret was sincere, and that was good enough for now.

Suddenly, uncontrollably, terrifying memories flashed through his mind of his deadly night in Niccone, and he was certain that his crimes that night were the source of his recent derangements.

His urge to destroy himself.

To destroy others.

Desperate, he stared over at the little Mantellata.

"Do you know what I've done near Niccone?"

"Yes, some of it."

Horrified that anyone knew his secret, Malavolti stared away, into the darkest recesses of the prison chamber, trying to force it from his mind, but it was impossible. It refused to be dismissed, as images from that night swept over him: his overlong conversations with the Franciscan, his uncharacteristic intoxication, his unnerving obsession with the young girl, his decision to leave the tavern, his murder of his squire and the priest.

Then he remembered the girl.

Maria Angelina.

She was standing in the garden, staring upwards at the distant stars. He attempted to spur his mount, to escape, but he was incapable. Instead, he watched her obsessively. Her long brown hair. Her perfect angelic face. Despite his drunken agitations, he took a moment to wonder what the young girl might be thinking about: maybe her betrothed somewhere in Genoa, maybe the Poor Clares whom she'd wanted to join, maybe just the beauty of the dark night sky.

Whatever it was, Malavolti had been irresistibly enflamed by the mere sight of the lovely young girl. He was overcome with the vilest of all human impulses, and he fought within himself, and against himself.

Without success.

Astonished, the dark knight suddenly found himself slumped to the floor of the prison infirmary, beside Alonzo's deathbed pallet.

He reached up and took the little nun's hand.

"Help me."

"God is merciful," she assured him.

"What I've done is unforgivable!"

"God forgives countless crimes and aberrations, many right here within these stone walls.

"Even if your God *could* forgive me, how could I forgive myself?"

"You can't," she explained, "not without God's help."

"What should I do?"

"Confess. Confess to the friar."

But the dark knight felt incapable of such a thing.

He had no faith.

After all, what would he be confessing to?

"Cousin?" she interrupted softly, and Malavolti looked up, stunned by the word cousin, which was, of course, true.

They *were* cousins.

"Yes?"

"Are you not aware that your penance has already begun?"

He seemed to understand.

"Last night?"

"Yes. The demon despises guilt, but he loves despair. He especially loves suicide. But in your own difficult way, you've somehow resisted. Now it's time to confess."

"I have no faith."

"Let the priest decide."

"All right," Malavolti conceded, with exasperation, "I'll do whatever you tell me to do."

But he felt certain that the little nun wasn't finished.

That she had more to say.

"What else, little cousin?" he asked.

"You need to work here for several months. Then you'll need to leave us and find the young woman in the garden. She'll need you then. So will her child."

Malavolti was stunned.

Horrified.

"A child?"

"Yes, the child in her womb."

As Malavolti tried to comprehend what had just happened, another tertiary, Sister Venturella, came into the infirmary.

Margaret looked in her direction.

"I'm sorry to interrupt," Venturella said softly, "but you're needed in the forward chamber."

Margaret understood, and she nodded. Then she reached forward in the darkness, found the knight's forehead, and touched him gently.

"Have trust. Have trust in God's mercy."

Then she rose on her crutch and limped from the chamber with Sister Venturella at her side.

The dark knight wasn't surprised by the terrible loneliness he felt without her. Especially when he glanced down at the blood-encrusted face of the dead Alonzo.

"Maybe God could forgive a creature like this fundamentally decent man," he thought to himself, "but how could He ever forgive a monster like me?"

A murderer.

A man who'd violated an innocent young woman.

A man who'd impregnated an innocent young woman.

A monster.

Malavolti didn't know the answer, so he sat in the darkness all night long thinking about it.

Staring down at the bloody corpse.

Chapter 14

Cousins

Città di Castello, the Papal States: October 1319

"But you were imprisoned," Malavolti reminded his cousin, recalling the tiny doorless cell he'd seen in the Metolan chapel. "I've seen that little hole they put you in."

"Yes, I *was* imprisoned, but I was imprisoned in the House of God."

It was late at night, and the cousins were sitting alone in the prison's interior courtyard. Malavolti had finished his labors for the day, and when the prisoners had fallen to sleep, he'd come out to the large stone well to sit and think beneath the silent stars. A week had passed since he'd arrived at the Castellan prison, and he was astonished at how easily he'd acclimated to his new life. Maybe his adaptability, he speculated, was due to the warrior mentality that had been ingrained within him his entire life.

For most of the week, Malavolti had done nothing but care for prisoners. He was constantly at work, and as far as he could tell, he hadn't undergone any kind of alteration in his thinking. He certainly hadn't experienced any kind of mystical or spiritual transformation, let alone a conversion. But he did learn to place his trust in the guidance of his little cousin, and as a result, he'd discovered a remarkable comfort here at the prison, despite its squalor, despite its sufferings.

He knew, of course, that he wouldn't be staying here forever. Margaret had made that perfectly clear. This period of his life was apparently a hiatus of some kind, and he was willing to be both patient and receptive. Even though he hadn't confessed his crimes to the friar as he'd promised, he still hadn't ruled it out. In truth, he hadn't ruled out anything. As for Margaret, she never mentioned it again. She was also waiting patiently. She was, it seemed, endlessly patient. She was also completely selfless in a way that Malavolti found hard to comprehend.

He'd also noticed that she seldom slept. Quietly, unobtrusively, she undertook all kinds of self-mortifications and fastings. She actually spoke very infrequently, always listening to others more than speaking herself. Unless she felt it was necessary. When she did so, she was always, without fail, perfectly cheerful, even affectionate. She also possessed, as Malavolti had recognized immediately, an almost luminous intelligence. She knew the scriptures, including the underlying theology, with a far greater depth than any of the university scholars that Malavolti had encountered in his past.

Earlier, after her prayers in the prison chapel, Margaret had decided to visit her cousin, and Malavolti watched her coming into the courtyard unaided, limping with her crutch, gently touching the walls she'd carefully memorized to find her way. Finally, she sat down on the stone steps and gazed up at her soldier-cousin who was sitting on the edge of the well. She was always a curious sight, so tiny in her Dominican white tunic and her long black cloak, with her disconfigured body and her strangely disproportional head. Yet her countenance, at least these days, seemed perfectly pleasing.

"Didn't you ever curse your parents?" Malavolti wondered out loud.

"No, I've always loved my parents. I was a child of six when they moved me into the chapel, and I was naturally confused and hurt by what they'd done. But I did my best to comprehend their shame. My father, as you know, was the fearless Captain of the People, a great hero, and my mother was an elegant woman whose beauty was legendary in Massa Trabaria and beyond.

"But the great *Capitano* was also excessively proud and merciless, and my mother was weak. Somehow, even at an early age, I came to understand these things, often with the help of Fra Cappellano who continually reminded me that God was my true and eternal Father. So I prayed for my parents. Ceaselessly. And I forgave them. Every night I prayed that, whatever might happen to me, they would someday die within the graces of God."

When Malavolti seemed unconvinced, Margaret explained at greater length.

"It's true that I've always suffered from my parents' shame at my deformities, but I've never allowed myself to hate them. Never. Whenever I was tempted by the demon, I would repeat the lines from Psalms 26, over and over, until the temptation passed:

For my father and my mother have left me;

but the Lord hath taken me up.

"Besides," she continued, "living in the chapel, I was able to attend Mass every day and receive the Holy Eucharist. I was also given daily instructions in the faith by the kindly chaplain. I was fully aware that Jesus himself had also been rejected by his own people, and, eventually, as hard as it seemed at first, I came to realize that every cross, every single trial, was actually an extraordinary metaphysical gift from God. An opportunity for spiritual development."

"Well, cousin, you've certainly been given many gifts," Malavolti said, without cynicism, and Margaret smiled.

"Do you know what Fra Cappellano once taught me?

"Tell me."

"The only deformity that God abhors is the deformity of sin."

She whispered it softly, and Malavolti thought it over for a moment. Then he continued with his previous line of thinking.

"What about the abandonment in Castello?" he wondered. "After thirteen years in your little stone prison, they cut you off with absolutely nothing."

Margaret remembered, and the memory was clearly difficult, but Malavolti pressed her anyway.

"Tell me about it."

"I was nearly twenty years old at the time," she remembered, "and it seemed, for a joyous day or so, that there might be some hope. Some hope that things might change in my life and my family. As you know, after a year in that underground vault in Mercatello, with no visitors, with no Mass, with no sacraments, I was finally taken, in secrecy, to

116

the cathedral right here in Castello, and I was finally allowed to attend Mass and receive the Eucharist. I was buoyant. Overjoyed.

"Then after Mass, I was taken to the tomb of Fra Giacomo, which was surrounded by a large crowd of petitioners, and I was instructed to pray for my healing. For a miracle of complete and immediate healing. So I did as they wished. Fervently. In truth, I had no idea what God's plans for me might be, but I prayed for His mercy and that His will would, of course, be done. The day passed quickly. It had been so long since I'd been in a church that I was exhilarated by the close proximity to the true presence of Jesus. Eventually, as the crowds began to dissipate, I grew concerned about my parents.

"At first, I worried that something might have happened to them, but, in time, I began to wonder if they were ever coming back. At vespers, as the cathedral bells rang out, a sexton reluctantly asked me to leave. When I'd finally hobbled outside into the night, blind and penniless, I could hear the heavy wooden doors locking behind me. Then I spent the entire freezing night waiting on the cathedral steps for my parents to return, but they never did.

"So I prayed that God would forgive them and that He would help me, a wretched outcast, who'd been rejected by her own parents. It was difficult, of course. Very difficult. It was the most difficult trial of my life, but I understood their weaknesses better than anyone else, so I forgave them, and I prayed for them. Later that night, I was befriended by two curious beggars, Roberto and Elena. At first, they tried to help me in the hope of some kind of reward, but they quickly learned from the guards at Porta Sant'Egidio that Parisio and his party had left the city. Then the beggars, outcasts themselves, took pity on my helpless situation and taught me how to beg for my subsistence, which I did for several years."

When Malavolti said nothing, the little nun changed the subject.

"Did you know that the initiation ceremony of a Mantellata is very similar to that of a knight?"

Malavolti had no idea.

"We swear fealty to a much higher Lord," she smiled, "but it's much the same: the vows, the prayers, even the kiss of peace."

"Are we both warriors, little Margaret?" the mercenary asked without condescension.

"We are," she replied, "but a Mantellata must be the most humble of the humble, and I'm afraid that tonight I've broken one of St. Dominic's many wise admonitions."

Malavolti waited for her explanation.

"The good saint once said that the truly pious 'speak only to God or about God,' and tonight, I've done nothing but talk about myself."

But the little Mantellata wasn't truly mad at herself, even though she was acutely aware that self-absorption is a serious flaw of the spirit.

"It's my fault, cousin, I've asked too many questions."

"Yes, but you're my *special* cousin, and I believe you have a right to know these things. My parents may have shunned me, then rejected me, but I understood their human weaknesses, and I've loved them with every single moment of my life."

Malavolti believed her.

"I can only hope," she added, "that God has assisted them in their needs. I'm told that my mother died last year with a priest at her side, so I'm hopeful. But I know nothing of my father's recent death in Montone."

"I was there."

Margaret was astonished, which surprised Malavolti.

She explained.

"I only know the things I'm *privileged* to know."

The dark knight nodded and remembered:

"As I stood at his deathbed, plotting to seize his estates, the dying warrior cried out to God for forgiveness. He called out for his child, and he begged for mercy. There was a priest at his side."

Margaret was overcome.

Her glazed and sightless eyes flushed with tears. Uncertain what to do, Malavolti stood up and knelt down beside his little cousin, who was, he was certain, praying silently. Gently, the dark knight took out his handkerchief and carefully wiped the streams of tears that dampened her face.

The little nun looked up into his eyes.

"You've given me the most extraordinary gift, dear cousin! This, I believe, is another important reason why you've come to Castello. To bring me comfort."

Malavolti was pleased. He'd certainly never thought of himself as a messenger of good tidings, but now it seemed to be the case, and he was perfectly content.

Margaret, with exuberant spirit, patted his hand.

Gently.

"God is good, Visco," she said.

With conviction.

Malavolti, even though he wasn't so certain about the distinguishing qualities of God, was delighted to hear Margaret call him by his childhood name. Except for Alighieri, no one had done so since his uncle had left for Portugal over twenty years ago.

Eventually, the little Mantellata rose from the stone steps, took her crutch, and began to exit the darkened courtyard.

"God bless you, dear cousin," she said softly, as Malavolti watched her leave. He felt certain that she'd spend the coming night in her freezing charred garret within Venturino's palace praising God, praising His holy Name.

Chapter 15

Sister Venturella

Città di Castello, the Papal States: January 1320

Malavolti washed the corpse of an old man, a murderer named Azzo, who'd died earlier in the night. Like so many others in this hideous place, the old man had died of the shaking fever. Malavolti was once told by the sisters that more than half of the prisoners died of the same debilitating delirium. This particular victim, Azzo, had suffered intensely in the final throes of the disease, but he'd also made his peace with God and died with the friar and Margaret at his side.

When Malavolti was done, he lifted the emaciated corpse and carried it to a portable pallet. Then he covered it with a cloth and sat down to rest. Since no one had come to visit the old man, surely no one would claim his body, so tomorrow morning Malavolti would bury the corpse in the prison cemetery.

Such burials along with Sunday Masses at the Cathedral were the only times that Malavolti left the prison, but he never complained. To his astonishment, he'd become quite comfortable here, working with the Mantellatas, serving these useless abandoned prisoners. So he bided his time, waiting for the moment when Margaret would tell him what he needed to do. To somehow help the young Pisan girl he abused in Niccone and the bastard child he'd conceived in violence.

It was now three months since the dark knight had stormed into this chamber with the intention of murdering the little woman who'd, so he thought, bewitched him. Much, of course, had changed since then. At least, much had changed in Malavolti. It was nothing obvious or dramatic. In fact, he was almost unaware that it was happening. But it had. Twice he'd attempted to write his friend Alighieri, but each time he found that he couldn't express himself adequately.

Frustrated, he'd recall the times in his life when good-intentioned people had tried to describe the full encompassment of their faith or their personal conversion, and how badly they'd always floundered. In those days, of course, Malavolti had dismissed them all as fools, but now that he finally understood what they'd been attempting to say, he found that he couldn't express it any better than anyone else.

All he could say for certain was that everything had begun with a simple trust in his cousin Margaret, that it had grown gradually under the influence of the Mantellatas' good example, and that it had finally, almost imperceptibly, ended with an astounding awareness not only of the presence of God in this difficult world, but His divine mercy as well. Everything had initiated from the trust which he'd placed in another person for the first time in his life since the death of his uncle. He'd also come to realize why it had been so difficult for a man like himself. Because it was akin to submission. Because it was akin to something he'd never been able to tolerate before. Which was also, he now understood, something akin to love.

Which was also a form of submission.

One dark night during his second week at the prison, Malavolti had asked his cousin how a man like himself could learn to submit his will to anything or anyone beyond himself, and she'd seemed quite surprised by his question.

"Like everyone else, Visco."

"Tell me."

"With prayer," she explained, as if it was perfectly obvious. "With prayer and patience."

Then she rose, hobbled away, and left Malavolti to think about it alone. But he was naturally uncomfortable with the notion of prayer, precisely because it was, in essence, a humbling. It was a submission. So he decided to be patient instead. A week later, as he was cleaning the terrible boils on the back of a young prisoner, he discovered, to his amazement, that he'd actually prayed for the pitiful young man. He'd done so almost unconsciously, whispering somewhere in the deep silence of his mind four simple words, "Christ, help this boy." On the surface, it might have seemed ordinary enough, but it wasn't, not for Malavolti, and he knew it. It was the first time in over twenty years that he'd spoken to God.

That he'd raised his heart and his mind to God.

In time, unexpectedly, it happened again. Then again and again. Eventually, Malavolti came to accept the possibility that God might actually forgive his crimes, that He might actually love him in all his wretchedness, along with all the other wretches of the universe. As a result, he felt an even closer communion with Margaret and the Mantellatas, and he finally went to Confession.

He began to see himself as a Christian.

Nevertheless, given his crimes, he still felt himself to be the worst and the least of all living Christians, but it really didn't matter because he now felt a peculiar, silent, but undeniable inner joy. He knew that it was the very same metaphysical serenity that had empowered his uncle and made the great Crusader exactly what he was. Malavolti, of course, had no such exalted ambitions, but he was pleased to be, in some small way, like the two people he'd most admired in his life: the Templar Augustus Damiano and the deformed little Margaret of Castello.

When he tried to write of such things to Dante, who would have certainly understood, they always fell flat on the page, and he'd rip up the sheets. Eventually, he managed to send the Florentine a brief note apologizing for his rude behavior in Ravenna, mentioning in a *postscriptum* that he was now serving a group of Mantellatas in a Castellan prison. He felt certain that the poet would comprehend.

Distracted from his thoughts, Malavolti heard hurried footsteps approaching from the outside corridor and he looked across the infirmary at his little cousin, who'd fallen asleep for a few moments, sitting upright in one of the chamber's wooden chairs. She looked as she always looked: serene, vulnerable, seemingly in perpetual prayer.

It was perfectly obvious that Margaret never really slept anymore, except for brief little naps that seemed to be taken in the most uncomfortable positions. Although he really didn't know for sure, the other sisters told him that Margaret did nothing but pray during her nightly stays at the burned-out home of the Venturinos.

As the footsteps grew louder and closer, Malavolti knew exactly what was coming, and he dreaded it. One of the Mantellatas whom he'd grown quite fond of, Sister Venturella, had developed some kind of growth within her eye socket. Like many of the Veiled Ones, Sister Venturella was a widow who'd joined the Mantellatas to more fully serve her master, Jesus Christ. She'd obviously done so with great fervor, high spirits, and true compassion. Yet despite her faith, the good sister was terrified by what the tumor might mean, and she was now returning from a well-known physician in Mercatello.

Malavolti was certain that the news would be unfavorable. He'd seen many growths and tumors during his military life, and he knew exactly what this one meant. Blindness, suffering, followed by difficult death. As always, he was grateful that Margaret would be here to comfort her friend.

Three Mantellatas suddenly rushed into the room, as Sister Venturella, terrified, fell to her knees before the little nun. Awakened by the disturbance, Margaret opened her unseeing eyes. Amazingly, she seemed completely awake, and Malavolti was certain that she already knew the doctor's prognosis.

"Margaret!" Venturella cried out, "Help me, dear Margaret! The doctor says I'm losing my sight, and I can't bear the thought!"

The afflicted sister was so upset that she seemed unaware that she was speaking to someone who was already completely blind.

"The doctor can do nothing?" Margaret asked.

"He could attempt a surgery," the older nun explained, "but he admitted that it probably wouldn't make any difference, and that it would cost much more money than I could imagine."

She broke down completely.

She dropped her head into Margaret's lap, sobbing. Pitifully. Gently, Margaret placed a comforting hand over the woman's head and looked up towards the other sisters.

"It's true," Sister Carita assured her.

"Please help me, Margaret!" Sister Venturella cried out, as she looked up, shuddering with fear, at the little nun's face.

"But sister," Margaret said softly, "God is offering you an extraordinary gift. You need to learn to accept it."

"I'll *never* accept it! Never! How could God be so cruel?"

Again, Margaret tried to reassure the suffering woman.

"What you gain for your difficulties will be yours forever."

"No!" Venturella cried out. "I won't accept it! Never! Never! Never! Please help me, sister!"

For the first time, Malavolti understood what the terrified nun was asking, and he was amazed. He also realized, whatever Sister Venturella's motivations, it was an incredible testimony of her faith in God and His expressions of earthly power through the means of her little friend.

The panicked woman clutched tightly to Margaret's deformed little legs, looking up into her friend's sightless eyes.

"I can't bear the thought of never seeing the faces of my children again," she said. "I'd rather die. I'd rather die!"

Everyone was greatly affected by the poor woman's desperation, and Malavolti, much to his astonishment, found himself wishing that he could take up the woman's burdens himself. Amazingly, without even thinking about it, he'd offered himself in her place.

It wasn't necessary.

Little Margaret had also been greatly moved, and she lifted up her right hand.

"Place my hand over your eye, sister."

Malavolti, who'd already witnessed numerous miraculous occurrences in Castello, still couldn't believe what he was seeing.

Margaret lifted her face, as if praying directly to the heavens.

Suddenly, Sister Venturella dropped her head into Margaret's lap again.

It was over.

Done.

Everything had happened quickly and casually, but Malavolti knew exactly what had taken place. The woman had been cured, and Sister Venturella and Margaret and the other sisters knew it as well, and they were already praying in gratitude.

The dark knight, overwhelmed by the woman's faith and God's amazing compassion, also praised a God that could do such amazing things. As he did so, Margaret glanced in his direction, directly into his eyes, and he realized that she *knew* that he'd silently offered himself for Sister Venturella. He also realized, in that single moment, that his time had come.

When Sister Venturella lifted her head, she spoke calmly to Margaret. Once again, she was her gentle humble self.

"Thank you, dear Margaret," she whispered, "please pray that God will forgive my weakness."

"God understands all our weaknesses," Margaret assured her.

Sister Venturella stood up. Then bending down, she kissed Margaret's cheek, and she and the other sisters left the room. From where

Malavolti was standing near the doorway, he could see Venturella as she passed beneath the light of a hanging lantern.

The once visible tumor was gone.

"Cousin?" Margaret called out softly.

Malavolti walked over to the little nun.

"Is it time?" he asked.

"It is."

It was time for the dark knight to go back into the world and assist, in whatever way he could, the pregnant Maria Angelina, but he was uncharacteristically afraid and apprehensive. He was a man who'd feared few physical terrors in his lifetime, but he was now terrified, not of danger, certainly not death, but of seeing, once again, the innocent young woman he'd damaged and violated.

"I'll need your prayers every single day," he reminded his cousin.

"I'll never abandon you, Visco."

"Never?"

"Never."

He was relieved.

Somewhat.

The little nun spoke again.

"Could we discuss things in the morning?"

Malavolti, who hadn't recognized the depths of Margaret's exhaustion, was suddenly ashamed of his selfishness.

"Of course. I'll see you at daybreak."

Then the dark knight started to exit the chamber for his sleeping quarters.

"God is good," she whispered behind him.

"Yes."

Chapter 16

Monastery of San Giuseppe

Pisa: February 1320

T he dark knight rode to the heavy wooden gates of the Franciscan Monastery of San Giuseppe on the south bank of the Arno. Just below Pisa. From within, he could hear the monks chanting at vespers. Halting his weary mount, Malavolti glanced over at his new squire, Antonio Capanna, and nodded. Immediately, the young man dismounted and tugged at the guest bells beside the gate.

Then Antonio remounted in silence.

The dark knight had grown to appreciate the young boy quite a bit, and he had to remind himself, from time to time, that Antonio, at the age of twenty, was no longer a boy, but rather a vigorous young man. He was the only son of a Castellan merchant family, and he was full of high adventure, but he was also, as Malavolti was pleased to recognize, devoid of ambition or materialistic cravings.

Uncommonly silent, discreet, and obedient, Antonio had proven an excellent traveling companion, but unlike the rugged Parenzo or the bold Lorenzo, the boy's martial skills were severely limited. He was definitely not a warrior, but like all the young men in the Papal States, he was reasonably adept with an arbalest. He was also, the knight had noticed, quite intelligent despite his reticence. He made his own judgments about things, but he kept his opinions to himself.

During the long journey to Pisa, he'd become fascinated with falconry. He not only enjoyed taking care of the peregrine, but he'd also developed a deep affection for the bird. In truth, Malavolti was pleased in every possible way with the boy's willingness to learn, his hard work, and his loyalty. He could see why Margaret had recommended such a promising young man.

"His main goal in life," the little Mantellata told her cousin before his departure from Castello, "is to make his parents proud."

She was exactly right.

As usual.

When the doorkeeper finally responded, the mercenary knight was escorted into the monastery's waiting chamber. In the meantime, Antonio tended to the horses, as Malavolti's message was taken directly to the abbot. When the chanting of the monks came to an end, Malavolti knew that he wouldn't have long to wait.

In Niccone, he'd been told the young girl's family name, but he'd subsequently forgotten it in his drunkenness. In his guilt. So he realized that the only way that he could find Maria Angelina was to speak to a friend of the monk he'd killed. He was aware that he was taking great personal risk in coming directly to San Giuseppe since the young girl had surely told her family that she'd been assaulted by a mercenary knight who'd then murdered the Franciscan, Salvatore Zampa. On the other hand, Malavolti was uncertain if the young girl had known his name, and he was willing to take the risk.

During his journey from Castello to Pisa, Malavolti had considered many times turning himself over to the Pisan authorities and answering for his crimes. The only reason that he didn't was Margaret's mysterious injunction that he needed to help the young girl. So he was determined to attempt that first.

God willing.

The waiting room was spare but well-lit. The walls were blank, except for a large, extremely realistic, wood-carved crucifix. Malavolti, who'd been dreading this interview for months, stared intensely at the face of the dying Christ and tried to accept whatever was to come.

When he heard footsteps approaching from behind, he turned around and was astonished to see a familiar monk entering the room. Zampa! The old priest, with a second scar marked across his face, glared coldly at the silent knight.

"Have you come to finish the job?" he asked defiantly.

"You were dead."

"No, I was left for dead. By a coward."

Malavolti made no attempt to dispute the accusation. Finally, the angry impatient monk spoke again.

"What do you want?"

"To make restitution."

The monk scoffed.

"Just go away and leave me alone."

"I'm sincere," the dark knight replied, "I've confessed my sins."

But the monk still wasn't impressed. He moved closer to the dark knight and stared directly into his Assisian eyes. Although unconcerned, Malavolti remembered that the belligerent Franciscan had once been a warrior.

"She carries your child," he said with contempt.

"I know."

The monk was astonished.

"How could you possibly know that?" he demanded in disbelief. "No one knows, except her parents."

"I was told by a saint," Malavolti explained, realizing how preposterous it sounded.

Zampa stepped back, smiled oddly, and laughed out loud.

In derision.

"It's true," Malavolti insisted. "I was told by Margaret of Castello."

Suddenly, an instant alteration overcame the priest, and he stared even harder at Malavolti, as if trying to size him up, to fathom his depths.

"She sent me here to help," Malavolti assured him.

Uncertain how to proceed, the elderly priest sat down in a wooden chair and stared across the room at the crucified Christ. It was clear that he knew about the little Dominican tertiary and her saintly reputation, but he was still wary of the violent man who'd nearly killed him in Niccone, and, even worse, had violated Maria Angelina.

"How could you possibly know Margaret of Castello?" he asked suspiciously.

"She's my cousin, and I've spent the past three months working in her service."

The monk grew intensely pensive, clearly struggling within himself. He continued to stare at the great crucifix, as if searching for guidance.

Finally, he relented.

"Her father" he explained, "has sent her to Sicily under armed guard."

"Into exile?"

"No, to have the child murdered."

Malavolti was shocked, bewildered.

"But it's still unborn?"

"Yes, the child will be aborted by a Saracen physician."

Malavolti was overcome. With nausea. With self-disgust.

With terror.

"It can't be!"

"It is."

"Does she know?"

"Yes."

Once again, Malavolti was horror-struck.

All these horrors had been created by his own despicable actions, and he fought against the easy temptations of self-revulsion and despair.

At the same time, he was outraged by the monk's apparent inaction.

"Have you done nothing?"

"I've been banished from the family's company, and I only learned the truth yesterday, after the ship had already left port. Tomorrow, I'm planning to board an even faster Genoese ship that's stopping in Pisa for cargo."

"Let me come."

Both men knew that the knight could do exactly as he pleased, but they also knew that he was asking for Zampa's permission. He needed the bitter monk to accept his help, so that they could work effectively together.

The monk wasn't sure, and he took his time answering.

"How can you be trusted?"

"I swear it."

Then Malavolti nodded toward the crucifix, adding, "before God Himself."

"Does God have meaning in your life?"

"Yes."

The priest thought it over for a moment, balancing his revulsion of the dark knight against what might be best for the young girl.

"Will you do what's right for Maria?"

"I will. I swear it."

"All right, then we sail together tomorrow afternoon."

The monk rose from his chair. As he was about to leave the room, Malavolti called after him.

"Bless me, father," he asked, "and forgive me."

The priest stopped where he was, gathered his thoughts, and blessed the dark knight who knelt down on one knee. When Zampa was finished, he immediately left the room, and Malavolti rose and watched him go. The Franciscan had said nothing about forgiveness, but the dark knight had learned from Margaret the virtue of patience.

Chapter 17

Celeste

The Tyrrhenian Sea: February 1320

A lone, the dark knight stood on the deck of the ship, as the Sicilian twilight was darkening into the coming night. The moon and its million stars appeared bright and close, as occasional breezes off the Tyrrhenian grew brisk and colder. Pensively, he watched as the Genoese ship, the *Celeste*, sailed beneath Monte Pellegrino on the northern coast of Sicily then tacked gracefully into the Bay of Palermo toward the dimly-lit city.

At the southeast end of the bay, in darkening dusk, the dark knight could see the sharp outlines of the Promontory of Zafferano. The cool night air was flush with the pungent yet pleasant fragrances of the coastal lemon and orange groves. Swiftly, cautiously, the sleek *Celeste* headed toward the great harbor of the Sicilian capital. Everything, he knew in his heart, would happen in the next few hours.

He was ready.

He looked out at the distant city for the first time since he'd visited Palermo as a child. His own mother, whom he'd never known, had been born and raised in Marsala on the southwest coast of the island. As had his Templar uncle, Augustus Damiano, who'd taught him about the legendary island's past, and he often wondered if there was a more unique place in the entire world than the island of Sicily. Once, it had been part of the Roman Empire, then it fell in succession to the Byzantines, the Saracens, the Normans, and finally the Hohenstaufens.

Last century, under Frederick II, the Mediterranean island had prospered as never before. Among other accomplishments, Frederick was a serious poet, a Crusader, and the author of the world's foremost treatise on falconry. He was called, even in his own time, *Stupor Mundi*, the "Wonder of the World," even though he was twice excommunicated by Pope Gregory, and even though Dante had condemned him to hell for cruelty.

Sixteen years after Frederick's death, sixteen years before Malavolti's birth in Assisi, Frederick's young grandson, Conradin, was ritually decapitated by the French usurper, Charles of Anjou, who then, disastrously, assumed control of the island. After fourteen years of capricious oppression, the people rose up during the Sicilian Vespers and murdered every Frenchman in Palermo. Then they invited Peter, King of Aragon, to serve as the King of Sicily, which he accepted.

At present, the island was still under Aragon's control, but the centuries-old bickering between Sicilian nobles had continued unabated. This was unfortunate for Sicily, but good for Malavolti's intentions. Palermo was a wide-open port, and allegiances were always dividing and shifting. He was confident that he could, rather quickly, locate Maria's ship, the *Asfodelo*, make his move, then get her off the island within a few hours. Naturally, he was hoping that he wasn't too late, and he tried not to think about the possibility. The Franciscan, however, felt confident that they still had time, given that arrangements would have to be made for the illegal operation.

As they'd traveled together from Pisa to Palermo, the monk had gradually begun to accept Malavolti's companionship and the sincerity of his intentions. But he was still wary, and the dark knight understood his concerns. Nevertheless, the monk was a Franciscan, trained to forgive, and the dark knight knew that the man was trying. As for himself, he did his best to pray for the young girl and her child, but it was difficult, given the depths of his guilt, to even think about the young girl and the horrors that he'd inflicted upon her.

Although fully cognizant of his own crimes, it still seemed incomprehensible to Malavolti that the girl's father, a wealthy Pisan noble named Enrico Sorella, would intentionally subject his daughter to the impending nightmare. He also wondered if the young girl's mother was party to the crime, but he found it too fantastic to believe, so he made the assumption that she hadn't been told.

Occasionally, the dark knight would think about Parisio of Metola, and he would wonder if the Capitano and Lady Emilia would have murdered little Margaret in the womb if they'd known of her deformities before her birth. Although he didn't like to admit it, he felt certain that they would have. Then he attempted to apprehend a world without Margaret of Castello, and it seemed intolerably bleak.

Intolerably hopeless.

Malavolti was a so-called "man of the world," a mercenary knight with long experience, who'd seen and perpetuated almost every kind of evil imaginable, but he still couldn't comprehend how anyone could kill an innocent child in such an insidious and cowardly way. When he was a young boy in the Holy Land, at both Acre and Ruud, he'd heard terrifying stories about Arab merchants who sold mysterious potions, appropriately called "poisons," often wine mixed with myrrh, pepper, and ammoniac salts, to forcibly miscarry a child from its womb.

Later, he learned that abortions were regularly practiced throughout much of Muslim society, especially in the harems and the homes of the poor. He knew of at least two books, Ibn Sina's *Qanum* and Al-Razi's earlier *Quintessence of Experience*, both of which described various means of aborting a child, including pessaries, in which chemical abortifacients were introduced directly into the womb through the birth canal, as well as deranged mechanical techniques such as binding the pregnant woman's body before striking her stomach above the womb with a wooden mallet.

Even the world-weary Malavolti could never have conceived the current monstrous methods of certain skilled Saracen physicians which Zampa had explained earlier this evening. Such an abortionist, having bound the woman in an appropriate position, would actually pass his hand upward through the birth canal, directly into the womb, holding a copper needle or a spike with a razor-sharp blade with a hook attached. Then, with mortal risk to the mother, he would methodically dissect the limbs of the living child in its womb. Eventually, with the hook, he would draw out the bloody dismembered pieces of the murdered child. If the mother was late in her pregnancy, the child's head would be decapitated.

Listening to the monk's description, Malavolti fell into disbelieving silence. He had no words to communicate the horror he felt within the depths of his soul, especially given that *everything* was his fault. It was his own evil transgression that had conjured these unconscionable nightmares. Sin, as always, had spawned further sin, and the dark knight had been the foul instrument that had induced Enrico Sorella, a man he'd never met, into his own unfathomable depravity.

"How could anyone imagine, let alone tolerate, such a monstrous thing?" he'd asked the Franciscan.

"In multiple forms," Zampa explained, "it was quite common in the ancient world, including the Greeks and the Romans. Both Plato and Aristotle recommended the practice of abortion to constrain the size of Greek families. Those societies, of course, were the same ones that regularly murdered unwanted newborns by leaving them outside, abandoned, and unprotected, to die the horrible death of exposure. Infanticide, it seemed to Malavolti, was the hallmark of a barbarian society, regardless of how many cities it might conquer, or how many poems it might produce.

"It was only the Jews, the followers of Yahweh and the Book, who were the true exception in the ancient world. Then, of course, the Christians as well, who from the very beginning, categorically condemned both abortion and infanticide. *Murder is murder.* Both the newborn child and the unborn child are to be regarded as the sacred creations of God. Tertullian, the most powerful of the early apologists, called abortion exactly what it is: *man-killing*. Murder. So did Origen, Hippolytus, and Cyprian.

"After the conversion of Constantine, ecclesiastical laws were passed to eliminate the pagan practice, and Basil, Jerome, Augustus, and Chrysostom all condemned it categorically. Basil of Caesarea explained that both the abortionist *and* the mother, if she willingly participates, were deliberate murderers, and Chrysostom referred to abortion as "slaughter." The temptation, of course, is always there, even in the Christian West, and the church has unequivocally guarded against it."

"*I'm* the one," Malavolti admitted, "who's created the temptation."

"Yes," Zampa agreed "but now, with the help of God, maybe we can prevent the further violation of the young girl and the murder of her child."

As the ship glided through the black waters before him, heading deeper into the Bay of Palermo, Malavolti recalled and pondered these things in the silence of his heart and his mind. Desperate, he looked up at the blackness of the nightsky and asked God to give him strength to do whatever was right and just. Then, lowering his eyes, he stared at the distant harbor of the great Sicilian city, and he vowed that no one else, while he was alive, would ever violate the young girl again, that no one would ever harm her child.

His child.

Chapter 18

Asfodelo

Palermo, Kingdom of Sicily: February 1320

L ater that night, Malavolti, Zampa, and Antonio spurred their horses down the deserted wharf, pulling up at the guarded gangway of the *Asfodelo*. As anticipated, they'd located the Pisan ship with little difficulty. Now they needed a few moments to size up the situation.

Unfortunately, there was very little time.

Up on the deck at the front of the ship, an armed Saracen warrior was standing watch, stationed outside one of the cabin doors that faced outward from the starboard bow.

Astonished, Malavolti turned to the Franciscan who'd also spotted the Islamic warrior.

"Is it possible?" he wondered. "Would they really attempt such a thing on a swaying ship? On a boat in the water?"

Zampa stared at the black waters of the bay.

"It's calm tonight. The movements of the ship are soft and rhythmic."

Malavolti had heard enough.

Incensed, he dismounted immediately and walked to the gangway at the rear of the ship, followed by the monk and Antonio. There was no time for strategizing. They might be killing Maria's baby right now.

As well as Maria.

"I have a question, young man," Malavolti said to the Sicilian soldier who was standing on the dock in front of the gangway, who seemed unconcerned by the approach of a Christian knight.

With a sudden flash, Malavolti unsheathed his sword, swung it to the man's left shoulder, and pressed the blade against his neck. It was perfectly clear that Malavolti, with the same exact motion, could have decapitated the man, and the young guard knew it, and he stood in the dark of the night, motionless.

Terrified.

"Don't make a sound," Malavolti warned him, "or I'll toss your head in the bay."

The young soldier carefully nodded his acquiescence.

Then Malavolti looked at his squire. Antonio, as instructed earlier, was ready. In his right hand, he carried his arbalest, and Scone, the hooded falcon, was perched on his left shoulder

"Gag him, then bring him along," Malavolti said, as he removed his sword from the young guard's neck and headed up the gangway. "If he moves, kill him."

Antonio nodded.

Although he wasn't a trained soldier, Antonio understood what was at stake tonight, and, if necessary, he was fully prepared to use his crossbow.

"And remove that hood," Malavolti added.

Referring to the peregrine.

As the dark knight made his way up the ramp, he could tell that the Saracen guard, who was still standing at the bow of the *Asfodelo*, hadn't noticed their silent boarding of the ship. He was also grateful that it was the middle of the night, since the deck was quiet and dark. Despite his sense of urgency, Malavolti took a moment as he stepped onto the deck to briefly pray to Christ for the strength he needed.

In all his endless combats on the various battlefields of Europe, Malavolti had never once considered the possibility of his own death, but tonight the possibility flashed before him, and he knew why. For the first time in his life, something truly significant was at stake, not just the meaningless quarrels of antagonistic nobles or the vain ambitions of expansionist commanders. Tonight, the life of a child, *his* child, was at risk, and he was uncharacteristically frightened by the possibility of his own death. Not because he feared death, but because he feared not being able to help the helpless mother and her helpless child.

As he crossed the deck, with the monk right behind him, a young soldier stepped out of the darkness with his sword drawn, blocking the pathway. He was a young Pisan soldier, and although not lacking courage, he was clearly intimidated by the huge dark knight glaring down into his eyes.

"Don't be foolish, young man!" Zampa whispered. "Step aside! We're here to save lives, not to take them."

The soldier hesitated.

"Unless it's necessary," Malavolti added.

Uncertain what to do, the anxious young man dropped his weapon and retreated across the deck where he disappeared into the darkness. Malavolti, despite his irritation that they'd been discovered, had no time to pursue the young man. Instead, without wasting another moment, he turned to the priest as Antonio and the gagged gangway guard arrived on the deck.

He told them what to do.

At the bow of the ship, the Saracen lookout was gazing restfully at the nightlights of Palermo. He knew that the doctor wouldn't take long, and he had plans for later tonight. It was easy money assisting Al-ben Hassin, so he leaned back against the door of the cabin and bided his time. Then, unexpectedly, he heard footsteps approaching from the fore of the ship, and he grew keenly alert.

He unsheathed his curved sword.

It was a Christian monk, and there was, in fact, nothing in the entire wide world that he detested more than a Christian priest. But the man was old, and he moved along slowly, feeling his way as he approached. As if blind. But the soldier was still uneasy. No Christian priest should be onboard this vessel tonight, especially given what was taking place in the cabin behind him. Cautiously, the soldier turned to the old man with his sword ready.

As he did so, the dark knight came up behind him and smashed the hilt of his sword into the back of the man's skull. There was a sharp quick crack, as the man instantly slumped forward into the arms of the Franciscan who laid him down gently onto the deck.

148

Satisfied, Malavolti looked at the cabin's wooden door which was surely bolted from the inside. Then, from the aft of the ship, he heard an ominous noise, so he nodded at the monk, who quickly went to check it out.

Malavolti would enter the cabin alone.

He didn't mind at all.

He dropped his sword upright into the wooden walkway, stepped back from the door, and concentrated his strength. Then he kicked at the door, approximating the height of the interior bolts. The crash was tremendous. The door shattered, and the bolts gave way. Instantly, Malavolti retrieved his sword and pushed the remains of the doorway aside.

But even the dark knight was unprepared for what he saw inside the cabin.

Maria, bound with leather straps at her wrists, her shoulders, her ankles, and her thighs, was lying flat, with her knees raised, on a long wooden table in the center of the room. She wore a soft white chemise, and she looked groggy, as if she'd been drugged.

Stunned by what he was seeing in front of him, Malavolti was struck by the horrifying thought that he might have arrived too late. Desperate, he glanced around the well-lit room. It was like a scene from one of Alighieri's circles in hell, but he didn't see any blood, thank God, or any signs of a dismembered child.

Spread about the cabin were pots of water, piles of absorbent cloth, and rows of various infernal instruments and potions. Strung on the port wall, there was a row of glowing lanterns that bathed the cabin in a soft, orange, hellish light.

When Malavolti first stepped into the room, the old abortionist had backed up against the far wall of the cabin holding a scalpel in his hand. The Arab doctor was old and wizened, and his face, it seemed to Malavolti, looked like the goat's head of Satan.

At the same moment, the young girl instinctively lifted up her head, and when she saw the dark knight standing over her, she cried out in terror.

"No! No!"

Then she slumped back down to the table.

Malavolti hesitated, but only for a moment. He glared at the others in the room. There were two more Saracen soldiers with their curved swords ready and an elderly female assistant. There was also a terrified older woman whom Malavolti recognized as Leonora, Maria's attendant.

Finally, the old abortionist, having sized things up, spoke softly in his own language to his two Muslim warriors. It was a simple command, and Malavolti, who'd spent his youth in the Holy Land, knew exactly what it meant.

"Kill him!"

But the dark knight never gave them the chance.

As the closest soldier lifted his weapon to attack, Malavolti stepped forward with a sudden sweep of his sword and slashed into the man's left shoulder. Grotesquely, the man's nearly dismembered arm flopped uselessly against his side, and he slumped to the floor, as everyone else in the room fell back in terror.

Then before the other Saracen could muster his resolve, Malavolti kicked directly into his right knee, and the soldier's joint cracked loudly with a sickening sound. Immediately, Malavolti stepped forward and smashed the tottering man on the top of the head with the flat of his sword, as the spent warrior collapsed to the floor.

Then he looked at Leonora.

"Undo those straps."

Realizing that the woman was paralyzed with fear, Malavolti cracked his sword against the side of the wooden table, which snapped her back to reality.

"Now!"

As Leonora began freeing Maria, Malavolti looked back at the abortionist.

"Drop it," he said.

Visibly quaking, the old man dropped his scalpel to the floor. Then Malavolti stepped forward, grabbed the man around the throat, and slammed him back against the wall of the cabin. Staring into the panicked eyes of the old abortionist, he gradually tightened his grip. Both men knew with certainty that the Christian knight, at any moment, could have snapped the old man's neck, and Malavolti felt that he should do exactly that. Believing that it was right and just. He considered how many babies he could save by killing this cowardly murderer. Nevertheless, he decided against it.

He knew it wasn't his place.

He also knew that Zampa wouldn't approve.

"Heal your injured," Malavolti said firmly to the old man, nodding down at the wounded Saracen who was covered with blood. "But if you cause any trouble, I'll cut you right down."

Malavolti released the abortionist. Then the old man and his female assistant began to comfort the wounded Muslim warrior. The dark knight was fully aware that many soldiers have survived such wounds, but he paid no attention.

He looked at Maria.

She was now sitting up on the table, visibly pregnant, staring at him strangely, still drowsy from the effects of the Saracen drugs.

"Get dressed," he said.

She made no response.

Frustrated, Malavolti looked at Leonora.

"Get her clothes!"

When she did so, the girl remained motionless.

Even more frustrated, Malavolti was determined, if necessary, to dress her himself and carry her from the ship. He reached over, grabbed a nearby container, and tossed some water into the young girl's face.

It seemed to revive her a bit.

Then he heard a noise from behind him, and he turned around to see Zampa entering the cabin.

"Five Pisan soldiers," the monk explained, "including the one who ran away earlier. They're waiting on the deck."

Then the Franciscan stepped past Malavolti to comfort Maria, giving her a quick embrace.

"Hurry, my dear! Dress quickly!"

The young girl was still dazed.

"Give me her cloak," the impatient monk called to Leonora who did so immediately. Then the priest threw it over the young girl's shoulders and stared into her eyes.

"Hurry, there's little time."

When Maria nodded, Zampa helped her down from the abortionist's table.

"Where's Antonio?" Malavolti asked.

"Where you told him to be."

"And the gangway guard?"

"We tied him up."

Satisfied, Malavolti looked down at the abortionist who was still tending to the bleeding warrior.

"Any trouble," the dark knight said coldly, "and you'll die tonight."

The old man understood, looked up, and nodded.

Then Malavolti left the cabin, followed by the priest and Leonora who were both supporting the still-groggy Maria.

As anticipated, there were five Pisan soldiers standing on the deck of the *Asfodelo*. They were armed, prepared, and determined, and they were blocking the path to the gangway.

When Malavolti reached the deck of the ship, his young squire, armed with his arbalest and falcon, emerged from the darkness to stand beside his master.

Behind them waited Zampa, Leonora, and Maria.

"There's another one on the far side," Antonio warned the knight, and Malavolti glanced into the shadows and saw a sixth man lurking behind the five soldiers.

"That's Sorella's retainer," the monk explained.

Malavolti understood.

Then he stepped forward to deal with the five armed men. As he did so, the Franciscan called out loudly to the Pisan soldiers.

"I've been sent here by the Monastery of San Giuseppe to protect this child," he said with authority. "Step aside and let us pass."

"No one passes," said the leader of the group. "We have orders from Lord Sorella."

"Are you aware," the monk explained, "that Sorella has sent his daughter to Palermo to have her baby aborted by a Saracen physician?"

The men were clearly astonished, even shaken by the monk's revelation, but they couldn't fully accept it.

"We can't risk prison on the wild tales of a meddling monk," the man responded. "We have our orders."

The monk pointed over at the sixth man lurking in the shadows.

"What I tell you is true," Zampa called out, "and Leopardi knows it's true!"

The soldiers glanced over at Sorella's retainer, who remained determined, giving no response.

"That man is the demon," the monk insisted, "who made the arrangements to murder the child."

But the soldiers, no matter how horrified they might be, couldn't risk countermanding their master's orders.

The leader looked back at the Monk.

"The girl stays on the ship."

"Then I'll have to kill every one of you," Malavolti responded, which clearly intimidated the wary Pisan soldiers.

The dark knight glanced at his waiting falcon, which stood unhooded on the left shoulder of young Antonio.

"This bird," he warned them, "will rip out the eyes of the first man that moves."

He whistled lightly to the bird, and the falcon's deadish eyes instantly flashed in anticipation.

In anticipation of prey.

The peregrine's back tensed in readiness.

Malavolti looked at the soldiers, and he raised his huge sword to his waist, holding it horizontally.

"Do something!" said the irritated retainer. "This man's trying to abduct the master's daughter!"

Suddenly, recklessly, the leader of the group lunged at Malavolti, followed by two other soldiers. Instantly, the peregrine leapt from its perch, spread its huge wings, and flew with staggering speed into the face of the commanding soldier. Right before contact, it spread its powerful talons and drove them deep into the eye sockets and forehead of the stunned soldier. He cried out in agony. Then even before he could raise his hands to his face, the falcon flew off, circled up through the dark night sky, and landed back on the squire's shoulder.

At the same time, Malavolti had dropped to a crouch and slashed his sword upwards at the second soldier, slitting open the surface of the man's stomach. Instantly, blood sprayed all over the deck, and the third soldier wisely backed away. Malavolti knew the nature of the man's wound, and he'd done it intentionally. It wasn't as bad as it looked, and the fallen soldier, although he'd never believe it as he writhed in agony on the deck of the *Asfodelo*, would certainly survive.

"Hold!" Antonio called out, addressing Leopardi as the man tried to slip away to the bow of the vessel. When the cowardly retainer ignored the boy, the squire raised his crossbow and fired a shaft deep into the right thigh of the fleeing man who instantly crashed to the floor of the deck. As he did so, his forehead struck the wooden floor with a loud thump, and he slumped into unconsciousness.

Everything had taken place in a matter of seconds.

Astonished, the other three soldiers warily drew back from the dark knight and his young squire.

"Can you swim?" Malavolti asked them, fully aware that most Pisan soldiers can swim.

"Yes," one answered.

"Then drop your weapons and leap off the port."

Instantly, the three men dropped their weapons.

"If you give pursuit of any kind," Malavolti warned them, "I'll slaughter you all."

They believed him.

When the dark knight nodded, the three men leapt overboard into the frigid waters of the Bay of Palermo, vanishing with three sharp splashes.

"Come, Maria," the old monk said from behind Malavolti, and the dark knight turned around and watched them pass. The compassionate monk. The relieved attendant. And the most beautiful young woman he'd ever seen.

Except for one.

Maria Sorella had suffered greatly, but she was still young. Malavolti knew that he could never undo the evils that he'd unleashed into the young girl's life, but he thanked God that tonight, at least, things had been no worse than they were.

Finally, he glanced down at his silent squire, and they followed Zampa and the others down the *Asfodelo* gangway to the harbor wharf.

Chapter 19

Marie Camille

Off Capri: February 1320

"Why not tell me?"

It was the monk.

Once again, Malavolti was standing on the prow of a Genoese sailing vessel. Lost in thought. He'd been up all night, and now the pre-dawn darkness was slowly retreating before the softly diffused lights of the unseen rising sun. The ship, the *Arno*, had passed the silent island of Capri and was now heading into the southern Bay of Naples.

Two days had passed since their escape from Palermo, and the young girl, isolated in her cabin with Leonora, was gradually recovering from her ordeal. Malavolti, of course, kept his distance, aware that his presence would be unsettling.

If not worse.

So he'd spent the last two sleepless nights praying. Thinking. Praying some more. He was doing his best not to abuse himself into some kind of futile despondency. Nevertheless, having seen the young girl visibly pregnant with his own child, all his previous self-disgusts had returned. Margaret, of course, had warned him that this might happen, and Malavolti wished that his little cousin was with him right here on the prow of the *Arno*.

Instead, the old Franciscan had approached from behind him on the deck.

Maybe Zampa was also having trouble sleeping. Or maybe he wanted to thank Malavolti for his service in Palermo. Or maybe he realized that the dark knight needed someone to talk to. It seemed to Malavolti that Fra Zampa had put his natural revulsions in abeyance, and was, once again, trying to be a forgiving Franciscan. As St. Paul had pointed out, it was the monk's rightful place to "admonish the sinner," but he was also obliged to forgive.

Even his enemies.

He was trying his best.

When the Franciscan arrived at the bow of the ship, he was sipping from a small mug of blackberry brandy. Then he took a seat on the deck near the dark knight, and he invited the warrior to speak his mind.

"I'm ready to listen."

Malavolti didn't turn around. He continued to stare outward into the Bay of Naples, watching the subtle presentments of the coming day.

"Would it sound too familiar," he said, "if I told you that she was the most beautiful woman in Paris?"

Even though he didn't expect an answer, Malavolti paused for a moment before continuing.

"Well, she *was*," he assured the priest. "Her name was Marie Camille Lucan. I first saw her on a perfect Sunday afternoon walking like a goddess through the royal gardens. She wore a sleek red gown of beaded silk, unembroidered, with an elegant red hennin. Within her thick dark hair, she wore pearl fillets that matched her rings and her earrings. Slender and graceful, she moved in the seraphical manner that the Tuscan poets envision in their dreams and describe in their poems, but which none of them had ever actually seen on this earth.

"But *I* did. On that singular day in Paris.

"Then, Franciscan, there was her extraordinary face! How should I attempt to describe it? Angelic yet sophisticated. With high cheekbones. With a red sensuous mouth. Her eyes, a shade darker than her thick brown hair, seemed a profound mixture of everything that a mysterious woman could be: private and thoughtful, yet worldly-wise, clever, and vivacious. She was, of course, given her dark hair and eyes, not the typical, blue-eyed beauty of the French fop poets, but she was recognized throughout the courts of Paris as the city's most beautiful and desirable woman.

"Needless to say, one look at Marie Camille that day amid those lush flowers, and I instantly forgot all the other young beauties in Paris that had previously aroused my interest. Immediately, I began a rather reckless pursuit of the unattainable Marie Lucan. These days, it might seem unlikely that I'd even considered such a pursuit, but when I was twenty-two, and when Marie was eighteen, I was very well-connected in Parisian circles and, I must admit, much pursued by the French ladies of the day who were never displeased with my rather unique, dark, Assisian good looks.

"I was also a highly-regarded knight, of noble blood, serving in the king's elite cavalry, and I'd maintained, what seemed to many, a mysterious connection to both the Knights Templars and the worldly Prince Rostand de Cornay. I was a celebrated warrior, having served at the heart of the French calvary, as well as a trained diplomat trusted by the king. I was also due, when I reached the age of twenty-five, a substantial inheritance from my father, a deceased diplomat, which was held in trust at the Temple bank in Paris.

"Despite all these things, not to mention my youthful confidence and chivalrous high spirits, I was completely astonished by the remarkable ease with which Marie Lucan succumbed to my advances. In no time, we were the most sought-after and talked-about young couple in Paris. We attended glittering balls, hunted with the king, attended ceremonies of state, and even played the new frivolous game of tennis. I wrote Marie a thousand love poems, and I worshipped absolutely everything about her, even her coquettishness, even her sharp tongue, even her proclivity to intrigues of every kind. Nothing mattered. After a few breathless months, we were married in the great cathedral.

"Then nothing, it seemed, changed with our marriage. I'd been fully accepted by her family, Parisian nobles who'd lost their wealth but never their rank nor pride, and Marie and I continued to live a fast and breezy life amid the Parisian aristocracy. Whatever flaws of character I recognized at the time, whatever her moral lapses, I paid no mind. I was smitten, and Marie Lucan Malavolti became, without question, the complete and single obsession of my life.

"Then a few months after our marriage, King Philip made his fateful move and all the French Templars were arrested by order of his deceitful and perfectly illegal 'Mandate of Maubuisson.' From that day forward, October 13th, 1307, everything in my life changed. Everything was destroyed. Not because of the Temple. Not because of my inheritance. But because Marie had changed. She grew distant. Disinterested and cold. She was often missing, and her whereabouts were unknown. All of my efforts to reconcile the problem, which I naturally assumed had been caused by something that I'd done, were met with lighthearted dismissals. But there was nothing lighthearted about it. Within a matter of weeks, we were totally estranged.

"In the beginning, I refused to believe that Marie's behavior had anything to do with the precarious status of my inheritance, which was clearly threatened by the crown's attack on the Temple. Everyone in France knew that Philip wanted to crush the order so he could commandeer the bank. If he did so, I would certainly lose my fortune, but I was still young, connected, and unconcerned. I had no doubts that I could make a living appropriate to Marie's needs and standards.

"But, apparently, she expected a lot more.

"In time, I came to realize that everything about our relationship and our marriage had been an elaborate deception on her part, and that *she'd* chosen me, not the other way around. She was a young woman without a sizable dowry, and no matter how beautiful she might be, she was an unlikely match for the French princes and barons. Feeling desperate at the age of eighteen, she chose, instead, a dashing young knight of apparent means to support her desires, do her bidding, and escort her around Paris. It's a hard admission to make, even now, and it drove me to violent rages. Even despair.

"From that exact day, October 13th, Marie also refused my bed. I was too proud to press the matter, but I was deeply hurt and damaged. It was especially difficult since we'd always looked forward to our private times together in the past, or at least, it had seemed that way."

The dark knight paused a moment, but he never turned around to face the patient Zampa.

"I believe," he continued, "that there's no greater evil that a woman can do to her husband, or vice versa, than violate their wedding vows in such a malicious manner."

The celibate old monk nodded thoughtfully, attempting to comprehend such a betrayal.

Saying nothing.

"Even back then," Malavolti recalled, "even as a lapsed and fallen Christian, I refused the demeaning comforts of adultery or prostitution. Although I must admit, I can easily understand how a rejected husband might be tempted into such evil entrapments. A callous wife, who behaves as Marie did, has little idea, or even concern, what harm she does."

Then Malavolti broke from his personal reflections and, once again, continued his narrative.

"So, Franciscan, the wedding bed was loveless and empty, and my marriage was hollow. I was desperate, but all my efforts to even discuss the problem were casually rebuffed. Then the worst that could happen finally happened. I was informed of a rumor that she was conducting an affair with her half-brother, François Lucan. At first, I refused to believe such a thing was even possible, but eventually I had to face up to the incestuous possibility, and I began making discrete inquiries.

"The rumor was not only true, but it was a relationship that had gone on ever since she was fourteen years old. Taking place throughout our entire courtship and marriage. To my further humiliation, I also learned that the affair, the 'liaison,' was common knowledge throughout the royal court and everywhere else in Paris.

"Everyone knew but me.

"It's impossible to describe my subsequent rage or the depth of my emotional debilitation. After a week of nothing but blackness and fever, I rode south to Avignon where, I'd been informed, she and Lucan were planning to rendezvous. I found them rather easily, and they made no secret of their unnatural affections, even in the city of papal residence.

"I came upon them sitting on the banks of the Rhône. They were having lunch together on a blanket beside the flowing river. Her blouse was unbuttoned, and red wine had moistened her lips and heightened her condescension. I can't, in truth, remember everything that she said, except that, in general, she laughed me off. Her immorality was open and blatant, and I was told to go back to Paris.

"However lightly Marie treated my appearance in Avignon, Lucan, though no less amused and arrogant, was fully prepared. His arbalest was at the ready. At best, François Lucan was a mediocre soldier, but he was rather adept with a crossbow. On that day, however, I had far less fear of death than I had of their leering condescension. Finally, insanely out-of-control, I unsheathed my sword. Instantly, the man fired his weapon and the shaft sliced through my left wrist and into my chest. At that precise moment, I realized that Lucan had intended to kill me all along. That I'd been, once again, 'set up' by Marie Camille.

"It was clear that Lucan expected his first arrow to sink deep into my heart, and he was frustrated that he'd have to fire again. Which meant, of course, that there would be several uncertain moments before he'd be able to do so. With my left hand still pinned to my chest by his first shaft, I stepped forward, raised my sword with my right hand and flashed the blade downward across his shoulders. With a tremendous violence. As a child at the fall of Acre, I'd seen Saracens decapitate Christians with two sharp blows, but I'd never, until that day, seen it done in a single strike.

"The man's head jerked up a bit, then toppled down to the riverbank. For some odd reason, his headless torso remained sitting perfectly upright on the picnic blanket. Without thinking about what I was doing, I sheathed my sword, bent down, and picked up the man's dismembered head by the hair. Then I dangled it in front of the terrified face of the only woman I've ever loved.

"'Would you like to hold your lover now?' I asked maliciously. I even considered dropping his blood-dripping head into her lap, but she fell backwards into a bizarre paroxysm, as her entire body began to throb and spastically jerk on the bloody blanket. Never once, did she scream. Nor make a single sound.

"Obviously, I'd gone too far in my demented cruelty, and I was ashamed of what I'd done. I also realized, although it hurt me deeply, that she'd probably loved the man. Uncertain what to do, I tossed his useless head into the river. Then I left her with her seizures and rode away with the man's arrow still protruding from my chest."

Once again, Malavolti paused, but this time he turned around to face the silent monk.

"A few months later she died in Avignon. I was told that it was a fever, but there were rumors that she'd taken her own life. A few months after that, I was exonerated by the king, who'd always detested François Lucan, and who was also fully aware of Marie's affairs and infidelities. Nevertheless, to satisfy the enraged French aristocracy, I was sent into exile.

"That same day, Philip condemned the fifty-four innocent Templars to the stake in Paris. I was there at the burning, and I saw them die, and it seemed to confirm my despair. My hopelessness. I'd already abandoned God, and now I'd abandoned any possible hope of love, of marriage, of companionship. So I rode off to war, the only thing that I could do better than anyone else, and I served in various military campaigns sanctioned by the unscrupulous Philip the Fair.

"When my exile was done, I returned to Paris in time to witness the cynical execution of Jacques de Molay and the final destruction of the Temple. Any lingering hopes that I might have harbored about my inheritance were gone forever. Immediately, I set out for Scotland, fully prepared to die in the brutal war with Edward II.

"Later, when I survived the Bruce's great triumph at Bannockburn, I left the Scottish wars behind me and traveled, for several years, all over Europe working as a mercenary knight. Always willing to serve, to kill, for whomever paid the most in gold.

"Eventually, I determined a new course for my faltering life. Abject cupidity. I vowed that I would, by one means or another, accumulate enough wealth to live out my life in comfort. Without God. Without companionship. But, at the least, in material comfort. I was actively pursuing that end when I first saw the frightened face of Maria Sorella looking out from her carriage on the road to Niccone."

Malavolti ceased his narrative.

Zampa seemed to understand.

"She resembles your dead wife?"

"Almost exactly. It's uncanny. Unnerving as well. When I first saw her face that afternoon in the carriage, everything in my entire life, everything that was bitter and evil and hopeless, somehow resurfaced. During our subsequent meal at the inn, I was completely obsessed with the young girl. Both attracted and repulsed. I knew it was irrational, of course. I knew it was unfair, but I was a lost man, wallowing in the confusions of my wasted life. Even after she'd retired to her room, my compulsive distractions continued throughout our late-night conversations, drinking far too much wine. Later, afraid of what I might do, I resolved to ride to Metola, but then I saw her standing in the garden. In the moonlight. I was overcome. I was also drunk, and I did whatever I did."

"You don't remember?"

"No, but I'm sure that *you* do."

"I found you standing over Maria that night, and I tried to intervene, but you beat me unconscious."

"Surely, you know what happened beforehand. You're the girl's confessor."

"Maria has never discussed the details. For weeks afterwards, she was too devastated. Then, after she learned she was pregnant, she tried to push it from her mind. So I've never pressed her to relive the horrors of that night."

Malavolti understood.

But there was something else that the monk was confused about.

"Why did you kill the boy? Your young squire?"

"I have no idea. Maybe, like you, he tried to intervene."

"I have something that belonged to that boy."

The monk held up a religious metal and chain.

It was St. Joseph holding the child Jesus.

"After you left, we buried his body, and I gave away his horse and crossbow, but I found this in his saddle bag, and I've kept it ever since. Maybe it should be returned to the boy's mother. It's engraved, 'Love, Mother.'"

Malavolti recognized the medal immediately, but he said nothing. He took it from the priest and put it away. He would deal with it later.

Still feeling the need to fully explain himself, he stared directly at the priest.

"I want you to understand that I'm not blaming what I did on what happened with my wife. And I certainly don't blame it on the wine. I blame everything on myself. On my cowardice. But I've wanted you to know these things. I've wanted you to know that never, in my previous life, have I ever abused a woman. In any way. In any fashion. Except when I tortured my adulterous wife with the decapitated head of her dead lover."

In the silence that ensued, Malavolti stared out at the bay. The dawn was now upon them, gradually lighting up the Italian coast south of Naples.

The monk broke the silence.

"Have you confessed these things?"

"I have."

"Do you believe that God has forgiven you?"

"I do."

"Have you forgiven yourself?"

The dark knight shrugged.

"I'm trying. It's especially hard when you actually see the ramifications of your transgressions."

The monk understood.

"Is that why you've told me these things this morning?"

"I've told you because I *needed* to tell you."

"Why?"

Malavolti considered how he should explain himself.

"Even though I wish it was otherwise, I realize that we can never *really* be friends, but I'm hopeful that we can be friends in Christ."

The Franciscan didn't hesitate.

"We are."

Chapter 20

Ship's Cabin

The Bay of Naples: February 1320

Afterwards, as the ship continued toward Naples, Malavolti returned to his cabin below deck. He felt comforted by his conversation with the priest, but he was confused by the religious medal that Zampa had found in the possession of Lorenzo Vasari.

His dead squire.

His distant cousin.

Malavolti knew the medal well. It had been given to Parenzo Greco, his previous and longtime squire, by Parenzo's mother when he was a child, and Parenzo had worn the sacred medal around his neck his entire life.

Then Malavolti's thoughts were interrupted by a knock at his door.

Probably Zampa again.

"Enter."

The door opened, and young Maria stepped into his tiny cabin.

Malavolti was shocked.

"You shouldn't be here, Maria."

"I *need* to be here," she insisted.

Concerned, the dark knight did his best not to look directly at the young girl, but he'd already seen enough. She was dressed in a long golden gown, looking perfectly lovely.

Looking pregnant.

He wondered if his mind was distorting his perception.

She spoke.

"I've done you wrong, dark knight. I've been unfair."

Which made absolutely no sense.

Malavolti waited.

"I've spoken with my confessor," she continued, "and it seems that you've been maligned."

"Me?"

"Yes. You've saved my life not once but twice."

"I don't understand."

She looked around the little cabin.

"May I sit?"

"Of course, forgive me."

Maria sat down in a small wooden chair and looked up at the standing dark knight.

"It seems that you have no memory of what happened in Niccone."

"I was drunk."

"You were, but you never assaulted me."

Malavolti was stunned.

He sat down on his bunk.

"Tell me."

"After that long day, after the brigands' attack, and the evening at the tavern, I found that I couldn't sleep. Naturally, I was grateful that we'd all survived the robbery, and I was grateful to you and your squire, but I had other things on my mind. Eventually, I got up from my bed and took a walk through the gardens. It was late at night, and no one was around, and I felt safe beneath the moonlight. I was thinking about my betrothal to an older man in Genoa, and I was apprehensive. We'd only met briefly, just one time, for about an hour, and although he seemed to be a decent man, I found that we had nothing in common. I also found him rather unappealing, which upset me because it seemed so superficial. But none of that mattered anyway since my father was demanding the marriage, and I was trapped, and I knew it.

"Unexpectedly, I was startled by the appearance of your young squire. We talked for a while, and given his heroics during the brigands' attack, I felt perfectly safe. Then he started talking about his forthcoming legacy, and he began boasting about himself and his future."

"His legacy?"

"Yes."

"Did he explain it?"

"No, but he claimed that it was coming soon and that his life would change dramatically. He was quite full of himself. Eventually, he grew more and more intimate, and I attempted to leave. Suddenly, he was all over me. Then he shoved a handkerchief into my mouth, and he violated me."

Maria hesitated, controlling herself, then she continued.

"I was a virgin, of course, and I was shocked and powerless. It was extremely violent and cruel, but I was strangely numbed. As if it wasn't quite happening, even though I could feel the pain, even though I could smell the liquor on his breath. When he finished, I felt his hands closing around my throat, and I realized that he was trying to strangle me. I tried to fight, and I tried to scream, but it was useless. So I prayed. To Mary in heaven. Suddenly, inexplicably, he flew upwards. Right off of me. Which seemed perfectly unnatural. Like a miracle. Then he flew away into the darkness, thudding against a stone wall, striking his head. Which made a sickening crack. I was certain that he was dead. When I looked up, you were standing over me, and I understood what had happened. I was still alive, but I was completely lifeless.

"You bent over me, a bit unsteady, and removed the handkerchief from my mouth. Suddenly, unexpectedly, you were attacked by Fra Zampa. Instinctively, you knocked him to the ground and beat him unconscious. Violently. Everything had happened in a matter of moments, and I was too traumatized to speak or even to react.

"Then you returned to me, picked me up, and started carrying me towards the tavern. But you'd obviously been drinking heavily, and you slipped, and we fell to the ground together, and I blacked out. When I opened my eyes, you were gone. I suppose that you'd staggered away in some kind of alcoholic confusion. So I lay right there on the ground in the darkness, staring at the stars in the sky, in and out of consciousness. I was sick in my heart, confused, physically damaged, and I wondered why I couldn't move. Eventually, Fra Zampa reappeared, stood me upright, and walked me back to the tavern. Where everything went black. For days. For weeks."

Even though she was clearly worn out from her traumatic memories, Maria was determined to press forward.

"Eventually, I was taken home to Pisa, where I did my best to forget everything that had happened, never discussing Niccone with my parents, or Fra Zampa, or Leonora. Naturally, I assumed that I'd never see you again, so I prayed for you every night. Then, like a miracle, you appeared in Palermo and rescued me a third time. It wasn't until an hour ago when I spoke to Fra Zampa, that I became aware that, for some reason, you believed that you'd raped me on that horrible night. I feel terrible that you've been carrying such guilts all this time, when you were the one who actually saved my life."

Malavolti was crushed with relief.

He was also surprised that the clever Franciscan had never figured it out, and he was also surprised that Margaret had never known the whole truth.

Surely it was part of his penance for his other reprehensible crimes.

He didn't care.

He now knew that he'd never hurt Maria.

It was the best gift that he'd ever received in his entire life.

"Thank you for telling me, Maria" he said, fully aware that the brave girl had just relived the horrors of that terrible night.

Just to do him a kindness.

Satisfied, the young girl stood up and walked over to the sitting knight.

"You've saved my life, then you've saved the life of my child, and I'm indebted to you forever."

She leaned over and kissed the dark knight on the forehead.

Then she left him alone in his cabin.

Chapter 21

Innkeeper

Abruzzo, Kingdom of Naples: March 1320

It was two weeks since they'd docked at Torre del Greco west of Naples, then traveled inland past the ruins of Pompeii, beneath Vesuvius, before arriving at the isolated Dominican Convent of Santo Paulo on the outskirts of Mariconda.

Zampa had chosen their refuge wisely.

It was distant from both Pisa and Palermo, and it had no connections with the Franciscans. He also had good friends, including a relative, among the kindly sisters. He was convinced that Maria's father, Lord Sorella, even if he were so inclined, would never be able to trace them to Santo Paulo.

Malavolti agreed, but he had other things on his mind. Once everyone was settled in Mariconda, he traveled alone to Abruzzo.

Leaving Antonio behind.

He traveled roughly two hundred miles to a small inn on the outskirts of Abruzzo, which is where his longtime squire, Parenzo Greca, had been murdered in his bed eight months ago. At the time, Malavolti had been finishing up some business with Berthold Oetker, and he'd sent Parenzo ahead to secure lodging. When Malavolti arrived, he was told by the innkeeper that his squire had been robbed and murdered, and no one seemed to know by whom.

Now the dark knight had his suspicions.

It was after midnight when he arrived at the inn, but he wasted no time. He barged into the bedroom of the innkeeper, an elderly man in his seventies named Guido Borso.

Needless to say, the man was terrified to be awakened in the middle of the night by a huge dark knight, who'd placed a small lamp on the table and loomed over the man's bed.

He drew his sword and dropped it upright into the wooden floor.

Frightened, Borso sat up in his bed.

He knew who Malavolti was.

He also knew *what* he was.

The dark knight glared down at the obese innkeeper.

"If you lie to me, I'll gut you like an animal."

Borso believed him.

"Tell me what happened the night that Parenzo died. Without any of the lies that you told me eight months ago."

"I was afraid to get involved."

"You're involved now."

Borso remembered.

"It was much like tonight. I was sleeping in this same bed when a guest suddenly entered my room and told me that Parenzo Greca had been murdered by thieves. I was naturally suspicious, but I was also terrified by the young man. He seemed dangerous, even unhinged, and for all I knew, he'd just murdered Parenzo."

"What happened?"

"He told me to hold the man's body until you arrived, then he gave me several gold coins to keep him out of it. I naturally wondered if it was money that he'd stolen from your squire, but I was too afraid to say anything, so I did as I was told."

"What can you tell me about him?"

"Not much. He was young and quite handsome. He was also French, with a French name."

"What name?"

He tried to remember.

"I can't remember his first name, but his surname was Sorel."

Which was a name that Malavolti recognized.

The dark knight lifted his sword and laid it across the old man's stomach.

"Anything else?"

"Nothing."

Malavolti believed him.

He sheathed his sword and left.

He would need to travel again.

Into his past.

Chapter 22

Renée Sorel

Tivoli, the Papal States: March 1320

T he dark knight was well-received by the Barone and the Baronessa, who fondly recalled his visit many years ago. He was offered quarters for the night, an enjoyable meal, and conversation with his gracious hosts.

At midnight, he waited in the garden.

Seventeen years ago, her name was Renée Sorel. She was just sixteen at the time, and Malavolti was eighteen.

Within the darkness, he glanced around the gardens where they'd once recklessly, foolishly, made love, as they'd done other times within his quarters. It was a few weeks after the French disaster at Courtrai, and he was convalescing for a few days with family friends in Tivoli. At the time, he was a self-assured young calvary knight, and Renée was one of the Baronessa's French attendants.

She was lovely, and Malavolti was a fool, and she was a fool as well. For involving herself with the likes of him.

They spoke French, talked about Paris, discussed French romantic poetry.

Guiot de Provins.

Colin Muset.

Then, just as she had seventeen years ago, Renée walked into the gardens past the hedges.

In the moonlight.

She was still lovely at thirty-three.

She was, as Malavolti had learned earlier, married to one of the Barone's military guard, with two children of her own, and highly valued by the Baronessa.

Highly respected.

"Visco," she said softly.

The dark knight bowed with respect, but there was no reason to waste time.

"Did we have a son?"

"Yes. The Baronessa sent me away at the time, and the child was raised nearby as an orphan, but I saw him regularly."

She looked at her one-time lover.

"But the boy grew up both embittered and violent. Eventually, he quarreled with everyone, even me, and the Barone sent him away."

She hesitated, then continued.

"I was afraid of my own son."

"He's dead, Renée."

Upset, yet not surprised, she sat down on the same bench where she and a promising young knight had once discussed French poetry.

"The wages of our sins," she said.

"Yes, but mine more than yours."

When she didn't respond, he pressed forward.

"Did you tell him about me?"

"*Never*, Visco, but he found out somehow, and he told me that he'd track you down some day and kill you. To gain his rightful inheritance. But I never took it seriously."

Warily, she looked up at the dark knight.

"Did he try to kill you?"

"No, but I believe he was planning to do so. He was using the name Lorenzo Vasari, and he claimed to be one of my distant relatives. I believed that he murdered my longtime squire, so he could offer himself for the position."

"Did you take him on?"

"I did, for a few weeks. He was mostly taciturn, sometimes silently brooding, but he was always ready for confrontation."

"Did you kill him, Visco?"

She spoke without accusation.

"Yes."

"Why?"

"Because he was strangling a young woman."

Horrified, she shook her head.

"Is the girl all right?"

During his trip to Tivoli, Malavolti had decided to conceal both the rape and the pregnancy from Renée. He was unsure what good it would do, and he planned, eventually, to ask Margaret what he should do about it.

For now, he left it unmentioned.

"She's alive."

"It's all my fault," she decided.

"No, it's all *my* fault, Renée. I was older than you."

"We were both young and foolish."

Which was true.

He changed the subject.

"Are you happy with your life?"

"I am. I have a good husband and two respectful children, as well as the affections of the Barone and the Baronessa."

She looked at Malavolti.

"And you?"

He shrugged.

"I'm trying to make myself a better person. Trying to make amends for my failures. My countless sins."

"You always had goodness within you, Visco."

"As always, you're overly kind."

Renée smiled and stood up.

"I need to return to my husband's bed."

She touched Malavolti gently on the shoulder, then retraced her steps through the garden.

Leaving Malavolti with much to dwell upon.

Yes, the dark knight *wasn't* the man who'd raped a young woman in Niccone.

Thank God Almighty for that.

But he *was* a man who'd killed his own son.

A son he'd barely known.

He was also the grandfather of Maria Sorella's unborn child.

Chapter 23

Convent Garden

Mariconda, Kingdom of Naples: April 1320

U nobserved, Malavolti stood on the balcony of his private quarters and watched Maria. It was more and more apparent, with each passing day, that she was carrying a child within her, and she seemed, if possible, to be even more beautiful than before.

During these past few weeks since his return from Tivoli, the dark knight had spent some time each day in the company of the young girl, but even more time observing her from afar.

This afternoon, as she did every day at this time, she was sitting in the convent flower garden at the edge of the olive groves. Her attendant, Leonora, waited nearby, and several Dominicans were working not far away in the olive trees. Maria, in thoughtful silence, sat on one of the stone white benches reading one of her devotional works. Zampa, with considerable satisfaction, had informed Malavolti that Maria was especially fond of St. Francis.

Especially the canticles.

Especially the letters.

Regardless of whatever she might be reading, this was the dark knight's favorite time of the day, and he always looked forward to it. From his balcony, he could observe her without being seen and nothing gave him more pleasure.

Sometimes, while watching Maria, he'd momentarily forget where he was, and he'd imagine that he was actually watching his young wife, Marie Camille, in the gardens of Paris. Then, realizing his foolishness, Malavolti would wonder what his life would have been like if Marie Lucan had been as moral and kindly as this remarkable young girl from Pisa. Unfortunately, it was a useless exercise, so he quickly pushed it from his mind.

During the past few weeks, something else had gradually been infiltrating his thoughts, and even though he tried to fend it off, it often managed to overwhelm him. The notion itself, of course, was fundamentally absurd. He'd begun wondering, in spite of himself, if the gratitude that Maria had found in her heart for the dark knight might somehow turn to love.

At first, he felt such thoughts were a violation of the young girl's privacy, but in time, he wondered if it might not be possible to salvage some kind of personal happiness from the damage done to their lives that night in Niccone.

"God works in strange ways," he would remind himself, trying to imagine the young girl accepting him into her life. Yes, she was supposedly still betrothed to a man from Genoa. Yes, Malavolti was considerably older than Maria. Yes, he'd lived a disreputable life. On the other hand, he was still young enough at thirty-six. He was also a capable knight, held in high esteem throughout Europe, and now he was a Christian.

He was also, of course, the grandfather of her unborn child, although he'd never told anyone what he'd learned on his trips to Abruzzo and Tivoli, except that Lorenzo had murdered his previous squire, but not that he was also Malavolti's son.

Originally, he felt it was simply an unnecessary complicating fact. Then, as he began to feel these powerful attractions to Maria, he decided to keep the truth to himself until he could travel to Castello and seek out Margaret's guidance.

As for Maria, Malavolti felt certain that he'd be perfectly content spending the rest of his life in service to this extraordinary young woman.

And her child.

With love.

Was it possible?

Only infrequently did they speak alone, and Malavolti was very careful what he said. What he revealed. At other times, at meals, during Mass, he silently enjoyed the pleasure of her company.

As for the others, he wondered what they'd think if they knew what was fermenting in his mind.

Zampa, he felt certain, would be outraged at first, but in time, maybe he'd appreciate the purity of Malavolti's intentions.

Maybe.

Regardless, it was a powerful submissive love. Nothing salacious. Nothing lascivious. If necessary, Malavolti would even be willing to forego the marriage bed.

Anything that she'd desire.

Maybe when Margaret once told him in Castello that Maria needed him, it meant more than just the rescue in Palermo.

Maybe.

So every night, Malavolti prayed on his knees that it might be so.

During the day, his thoughts again turned to Tuscan love poetry, especially the early sonnets of his friend Alighieri, especially the lines from *La Vita Nuova*:

> *My lady carries love within her eyes,*
> *and all she looks upon is made more fair.*

In time, the dark knight found himself conjuring stratagems for gently wooing Maria to his favor, without making her uncomfortable in any way. Even though he never actually pursued such thoughts.

Below in the convent gardens, Zampa had joined Maria at the benches, and several of the nuns also took a break from their labors to join them. They conversed with pleasure, laughing at the monk's good humor, enjoying themselves in the late afternoon sun. Malavolti wondered if he should join them, but he decided against it. Even during the frivolous years of his youth in Paris, he'd always been an outsider. Someone who was apart and different.

Which he didn't mind.

So the dark knight watched his new friends from his balcony, enjoying their enjoyment.

Then young Antonio, as he did every day at this time, arrived with the falcon, and Maria began feeding the predatory creature with little scraps of meat. She'd grown very fond of the peregrine, and she and Antonio enjoyed spoiling the bird-of-prey. Which seldom hunted anymore. Which often went unhooded. Malavolti's warrior falcon had clearly lost its fighting edge, but it seemed quite comfortable with its more peaceful existence.

So be it.

Then the group laughed again at something the Franciscan said, and Malavolti reflected on how much he admired the man. Within his own heart, he wished that he could emulate such an extraordinary person.

Who loved God.

Who loved everyone.

Even him.

After Malavolti's revival in Castello, he constantly thanked God for his rebirth under Margaret's care. Now he prayed, just as intensely, for the seemingly impossible: to serve, with love, the happy young girl beneath him in the garden.

Suddenly, the clear skies cracked and thundered, and a teeming sunshower fell over Santo Paulo. Everyone in the gardens below, laughing at the capriciousness of the weather, rushed to the convent for shelter. Only Antonio stayed where he was, with the peregrine now mounted on his shoulder.

Antonio stood there alone, watching the others leave, but, in particular, he was watching Maria. Despite the rush of the falling rain, Malavolti could see his squire quite clearly from his position on the balcony. Then, unexpectedly, the dark knight recognized something in the young man's eyes, and a sudden powerful pain surged within his chest. Instantly, Malavolti stepped backwards into his quarters, pressing himself, breathlessly, against the inner wall.

He was stunned.

He was completely overwhelmed by what he'd seen in the young man's eyes. It was, without doubt, the look of young love, and it horrified the dark knight much more than anything he'd ever seen on the battlefields of Europe. How had he been such a fool? How had he been so blind? The young boy had fallen hopelessly in love with Maria right beneath his eyes, and Malavolti wondered with trepidation whether Maria had, in any way, reciprocated.

As he considered the possibility, a terrible rage rose within him, and, momentarily, he considered seizing his sword, leaping from the balcony, and murdering the helpless boy down in the garden.

He managed to catch himself.

What was wrong with him?

He thought he'd put such violent feelings behind him.

Besides, it wasn't the boy's fault.

Why shouldn't he feel the way he does?

Maybe the safest solution was to send his young squire away. Tomorrow morning. But the dark knight knew in his heart that it was an inadequate solution if Maria had already responded to Antonio's attentions.

On the surface of things, it seemed perfectly ludicrous: a simple squire from the lower merchant class desiring the daughter of a Pisan nobleman. But that particular nobleman, as Zampa had anticipated, had disowned his daughter and cast her off without recognition or dowry.

Now anything was possible.

Even a squire from Castello.

In a rage, oddly confused, Malavolti slammed his head back into the stone wall trying to maintain control of himself, trying to think more clearly. But he couldn't. Nevertheless, he was fully aware that if he truly desired to serve Maria Sorella, to love her, he would have to submit to her wishes, whatever they might be.

It was little comfort.

With a single look, Antonio had unintentionally threatened all the hopes and dreams that had consumed the dark knight's interior life for the past few weeks. Everything had crashed around him, and he had no idea what to do.

He was also fearful of the violence in his heart.

Momentarily, he attempted to pray for God's guidance, but nothing seemed to happen. Then, suddenly, he realized what he needed to do. He needed help. He needed to go to Castello.

He needed to go to his cousin.

To Margaret.

Even though he was fearful of leaving his squire behind with Maria, he was also fearful of taking him along. So within the hour, without informing anyone, the dark knight mounted his horse and left Mariconda alone for the long journey north to Città di Castello.

Chapter 24

Chiesa della Carità

Trestina, the Papal States: April 1320

"**M**argaret!"

Malavolti could hear his voice crying out in the darkness.

It sounded strange.

It sounded remote, as if calling from the midst of the terrible fevers that had racked him all night long.

It had been a long ugly night of excruciating pain, nauseas, and the infernal heats of a fever. During most of the night, he'd been awake, drifting in and out of consciousness, tormented by his racing, relentless, unfocused mind.

He was lying in the upper room of a small tavern in Trestina, a few miles south of Castello. Several days ago, he'd left the Dominican convent in Mariconda and made his way north though the center of the Italian peninsula into the Papal States. But he'd pressed himself too hard, paying little attention to his wellbeing.

After all, Malavolti was a warrior, and he hadn't been sick since he was a child.

Near Avezzano, he hit a hard and sleeting rain, but he refused to stop. Foolishly, he'd driven his weary mount forward into the chilling storm. By the time he arrived at Craxi's laboratory in Niccone, he was deep in the sweats.

Regardless, the dark knight needed to confront the old man before he continued north. Several months ago, from Castello, he'd written the professor to terminate their collaboration. Unconcerned about the gold he'd left with the old man, Malavolti instructed Craxi to retain a fair portion for his time and expenses, and to donate the rest to one of the local churches. Specifically for the poor. Now that Malavolti was passing through the area again, he wanted to verify that Craxi had done as he'd been told to do. He was also concerned that the old man might be pressing ahead with the research that Malavolti had initiated.

It was, of course, the man's legal right to do whatever he wanted to do, and the weary knight knew better than anyone else that progress with armaments is always inevitable and unstoppable. In truth, Malavolti wasn't even certain whether such progress was inherently evil because he was fully aware that sophisticated armaments can be used to serve the good as well as the bad. Nevertheless, at this point in his life, he wanted no part of it. He was determined to leave his unscrupulous schemes behind.

As always, Craxi greeted Malavolti with respect. Yet reserve. The old man clearly felt betrayed, and the dark knight understood his position. When questioned, the professor claimed that he'd given the gold to a nearby church, and even though Malavolti didn't believe him, he didn't press the matter. He was more than satisfied to see that the man's laboratory was now being used for other purposes than the refinement of black-powder and the crafting of inventive weaponry. When the feverish Malavolti was ready to leave, he invited the old man to come to Castello and meet his cousin, but Craxi scoffed at the idea.

"I have better things to do."

"No, you don't."

An awkward silence ensued.

Then Malavolti rode off into the darkness again, leaving the old man and his workplace behind. Almost immediately, the fever fell over him with all its force, and he actually had difficulty remaining upright in his saddle. Several times, he blacked out as he proceeded, until he finally toppled from his charger just north of Niccone. Somehow, although he's not sure how, he must have staggered to a local tavern.

Throughout his fevered night, Malavolti was attended by various strangers who took turns sitting at his bedside. He wondered, on several occasion, whether they assumed that he was going to die, but he never asked. Actually, he never spoke at all. Within his tortured mind, all kinds of memories and strange conjurings swirled wildly, as he slipped back and forth, in and out of the blackness.

Most of the time, he thought about Margaret. Or Maria. Or the child. Sometimes he thought about his childhood in the Holy Land. He remembered the father who was seldom there, and the Templar uncle who often was. Even in his deliriums, Malavolti was determined to give his grandchild what his father had never been able to give to him, but what Augustus Damiano had: companionship, moral example, and a sense of intellectual curiosity. Then, irrationally, without sequence, he would think of his young squire and Maria and his own sinful past, and the fever would enflame and rage within him.

It was nearly dawn.

Even though he was still flush with the sweats, the worst was definitely over, but Malavolti was certain that none of his underlying torments of the soul could ever be fully mitigated until he was, once again, sitting at the feet of his little cousin. Where little Margaret would comfort him. Where she would guide him. Malavolti knew that he was engulfed in yet another war against despair, and he was desperate for his little Margaret.

Despite the concerns of the elderly woman who was sitting at his bedside, Malavolti rose from his bed, wiped his face, and left the tavern. He could be in Castello in less than two hours.

But things in Castello would never be as he hoped they'd be.

When the dark knight arrived at the city, there were no beggars at the gates, and he instantly knew that something was wrong. Maybe, he speculated, there was some kind of municipal ceremony in the piazza that might have induced the beggars to move inside the city. But he doubted it, and he assumed that their absence was an ominous sign. This was further reinforced by the fact that there were no Castellan soldiers at their posts in the guard towers. Finally, as he passed through the open gates, the city itself seemed deserted, so he forced himself to be patient, to contain his mounting apprehensions.

As Malavolti approached Chiesa della Carità, Margaret's favorite church, he could see a huge multitude overflowing into the streets from the open doorways. Everyone was silent, as they gently pressed forward, as best they could, to see inside the packed church.

Instantly, like a premonition, Malavolti knew what had happened, and his whole sickened body flushed with black desperation. Pressing forward, he rode to the fringes of the crowd and spoke to one of the mourners, a grieving woman.

"What's happened?"

She responded respectfully, without looking up.

"Saint Margaret is dead."

Malavolti said nothing.

He was overcome with loneliness.

He also felt, although he was ashamed to admit it, abandoned and betrayed.

After riding to the side of the church, he dismounted with difficulty and entered through the clerics' door. The inner sacristy was tightly crowded with priests and other religious, but no one questioned the presence of the tall, imposing, weary dark knight. Allowed to pass, he took a place near the front of the church amid a crush of standing parishioners.

In front of the altar, with her dark cloak for a shroud, lay the deformed body of his cousin resting on a wooden frame. As the funeral Mass came to an end, the Mantellatas, kneeling before the dead body of their sister, held up flaming candles. In the glow of the golden light, Malavolti could see Margaret's face for the first time. She appeared not only tranquil, but rapt with the fire of God's love. She seemed beautiful. There was even a slight smile on her face, and Malavolti believed that his sightless cousin had actually seen God's paradise during the last few moments of her life on earth.

When the final Latin hymn was sung, six Dominican friars, serving as pallbearers, walked over to Margaret, knelt down, gripped her wooden pallet, and lifted her up. It was clear that they intended to carry her body outside, through the church's side door, for burial in the cloister.

Suddenly, a determined voice cried out from the crowd.

"Entomb her in the church! She's a saint!"

Immediately, the church resounded with supporting cries from the people of Castello. They seemed horrified by the possibility that their little saint should be taken from the church she loved so much and buried like everyone else. Malavolti, in a kind of numbed astonishment, watched the increasing chaos in silence. He understood the feelings of the people, and he certainly agreed, but he also knew that Margaret would never have wanted special treatment.

Finally, the Dominican prior who'd celebrated the funeral Mass, stepped to the pulpit, and the uproar respectfully fell into silence.

"Dear friends, I also believe that Margaret was one of God's special people, but we shouldn't do anything that might jeopardize her case for sainthood in Rome. The church needs time to investigate, and we need to do everything in the proper way."

He was perfectly sincere, but he'd done nothing to change the minds of the people. Immediately, a rather sophisticated man named Orlando Orsini stood up and called out to the pulpit. Malavolti had once met the man when Orsini had visited an inmate in the Castellan prison, and the dark knight had learned that Orsini had once served as a professor of civil law at the prestigious university in Bologna.

"How long will the Vatican take?" he asked.

The prior did his best to put things in a hopeful light.

"St. Francis was canonized within two years of his death, and Anthony of Padua within a single year. We need to be patient."

The professor knew better.

"Albert the Great, Thomas Aquinas, and Margaret of Hungary have all been dead for over a half a century, and Rome is *still* investigating their cases. I believe that we should bury Margaret in the church that she loved!"

The subsequent outcry from the crowd was deafening. Malavolti had never seen anything like it before, certainly not within the confines of a church. The prior, aware that he couldn't sway the people with reason, nodded at the Dominican pallbearers who immediately started towards the side door, carrying Margaret on her wooden pallet. Immediately, the packed crowd of parishioners shifted itself to block the entrance, refusing to budge. Some were even threatening the priests with their fists upraised in anger.

Aware that his cousin would have been horrified by such a clamor in the House of God, the weary knight stepped forward to try and assist in some way, but he had no idea what he should do. Or what he should say. As he stepped forward, the frustrated friars backed away from the crowd, gently placing Margaret down at the center of the altar rail.

Suddenly, the crowd in the main aisle gave way to a peasant man and his wife who were, rather meekly, trying to carry their child through the tightly packed mass of parishioners. The young girl was obviously lame, and her father was carrying her within his arms. She seemed to be about thirteen years old, and Malavolti could see that her spine was severely deformed and curved. Both sickly and emaciate, the young girl had a peculiar look on her face, as if she was totally impervious to everything that was going on around her.

Malavolti, standing above the corpse of his beloved cousin, looked at the friars.

"Is she deranged?"

"No," one of the younger friars explained, "but she's deaf and mute. Deformed as well."

By now, everyone in the church had focused full attention on the struggling parents and their damaged child. Everyone watched in the silence as the father gently laid his young daughter down on the tiled floor next to Margaret.

"Blessed Margaret," the distraught mother cried out, "ask God to repair our unfortunate child."

The woman lifted her arms to heaven, praying silently. Powerfully affected, everyone else in the church prayed as well, including the Dominicans, including the Mantellatas.

Everyone was praying for a miracle.

But Malavolti was concerned. He remembered that Margaret's own parents, seventeen years ago, had brought her into this same church to ask for a miracle. For a cure. But nothing had happened. Now the dark knight was concerned about what might happen if the mother's cry went unanswered.

He glanced down at the floor, at the serene face of the cousin he loved, and he heard himself whisper, somewhere in the back of his mind.

"Can you help her, dear cousin?"

Then Malavolti, like everyone else, witnessed the impossible.

Margaret's arm rose, reached over, and touched the damaged child.

Suddenly, the young girl sat up. Unaided. She seemed stunned, as if momentarily confused. Then she stood up next to her mother and father who heard their daughter speak for the first time.

"I've been cured!" she cried out, overcome with joy.

Immediately, the church exploded into a wild yet pious exaltation of God, His power, and His little servant Margaret. The healed girl embraced her parents, and the prior pointed to a recessed chapel near the main altar. Immediately, the Dominican friars transported Margaret's body to the small chapel and laid her down in full view of the people of Castello. Everyone seemed satisfied.

Everyone was jubilant.

Malavolti was pleased as well, but he still had no idea what to do with himself. How could he deal with his own intractable problems? Margaret was dead, and he felt totally lost.

Alone.

Then he felt an odd compulsion.

He stepped over to the young girl, who instantly turned around to greet him, as if expecting him.

"Return to Mariconda," she said.

Malavolti was stunned.

He knew it was a message from Margaret herself, and he realized that something must be terribly wrong. He was terrified. For Maria. For the child.

"Be brave, good knight," the young girl said with compassion, "and hurry."

Then, as if nothing had happened, she turned back to her confused but overjoyed parents.

Malavolti glanced down at the dead body of his cousin, said a brief prayer of thanksgiving, and exited the church through the sacristy.

Chapter 25

Bedchamber

Mariconda, Kingdom of Naples: April 1320

Having arrived from Castello, Malavolti rushed down a dark corridor and found the priest sitting on a wooden bench in the hallway.

"What's happening?"

Zampa, greatly concerned, was staring at the nightsky through an open window. Probably seeing nothing. Looking as if he'd been praying for hours.

He looked up at the exhausted dark knight, who loomed above him.

"The child's coming tonight," he explained.

Malavolti was stunned.

"Too soon?"

"Yes."

For a few moments, they listened together to the sounds of childbirth coming from the chamber at the end of the hallway.

The sounds ceased.

The men waited fearfully.

Throughout his long life, Salvatore Zampa had been a man of the widest possible experience. As a priest, he'd baptized hundreds of children. But, in truth, he knew very little about birth itself. All he knew was that it was painful and dangerous.

Malavolti was equally ignorant.

Nevertheless, both men were certain that when a mother's labor ceased, the cry of the newborn child should be heard.

Not silence.

With trepidation, both men stared down the dimly-lit corridor to the closed door of Maria's bedchamber. Waiting near the door, young Antonio leaned on the opposite wall in his own silent vigil. When he saw the dark knight, he nodded respectfully.

The silence was terrible.

Where was the cry of the newborn child?

Malavolti refused to consider the possibility that the child was dead. The young girl had already suffered too much.

Then the child cried out.

Relieved, Malavolti looked down at the priest to make sure that he hadn't imagined the cry of the child.

The look on Zampa's face confirmed the good news.

"Thank God," the monk said.

Together, they continued to wait.

Zampa looked up at the weary knight.

"Where have you been?"

It wasn't an accusation.

"Castello."

The monk nodded.

Naturally, Zampa had been wondering about Malavolti. He had no idea why the dark knight had suddenly vanished. He wondered if Malavolti had felt out of place at the convent. Or maybe he had pressing business elsewhere. Or maybe, as it turned out, he'd gone to visit his cousin in Castello. But the priest had no idea since the dark knight had left without saying goodbye.

To anyone.

The door to the bedchamber opened, and the physician came out.

Malavolti remained where he was, but the old Franciscan rose with renewed hopes, walking to the door of the chamber.

From the look on the doctor's face, it was perfectly clear that something was wrong, and the other men braced themselves, waiting for the doctor to close the door behind him.

Malavolti grew impatient.

"What's wrong?"

"The child's sickly. *Very* sickly. Her eyes are useless. She'll definitely be blind."

"Will she live?" Zampa asked.

"I'm not sure."

The impatient monk opened the door and entered the room.

Malavolti followed.

Maria Angelina, bathed in the glow of the lantern lights, was slightly propped up in her huge white bed. She was holding a tiny child within her arms. Both she and her newborn looked beautiful beyond expressibility. Angelic, it seemed to Malavolti. As he drew closer, he could see the tears on the young girl's face, and he assumed that they were tears of both joy and concern. But Maria had already overcome her fears, and she looked up at her dear friend, the old Franciscan.

"She's my angel of God."

"She is," he agreed.

Zampa bent over and kissed Maria's forehead.

"You're *both* my angels," he insisted, and Maria smiled.

"I'll protect her always," she said softly.

"Yes," he agreed.

"So will I."

It was the gentle voice of the young squire standing behind Malavolti. The priest was surprised that Antonio had entered Maria's bedchamber uninvited.

But he didn't seem angry, just surprised.

"I'm not sure you should be here right now," he said.

"But I'd like him to be here, father," Maria insisted.

Then the young squire stepped forward.

It seemed to Malavolti that the priest realized for the first time what the dark knight already knew, that Antonio had fallen in love with Maria Sorella.

When Maria lifted her hand, Antonio took it gently.

Now Malavolti realized that what he'd been fearing more than anything else was true. Their feelings were mutual.

Antonio looked down at the child in Maria's arms.

"She *is* an angel," he said.

Then Malavolti, unnoticed, backed away to the chamber door.

"So *this* is what God has planned!" he thought to himself.

But his thoughts were disturbed by a slight and rather feeble sound that rose from the tiny child at Maria's breast, and the dark knight realized that the monk would need to baptize the newborn as soon as possible.

Then he left the bedchamber.

Silently.

Chapter 26

The Child

Mariconda, Kingdom of Naples: April 1320

Exhausted, Malavolti spent the entire night in the convent chapel. It was difficult.

Although not for the reason that he might have expected.

For some inexplicable reason, seeing Maria and Antonio together, lovingly holding hands, had tempered his soul, had convinced him that they were meant for each other. All of his jealousies, passions, angers, and foolish romantic notions were gone.

Maybe it was because his cousin was praying for him in heaven.

Maybe it was because he'd seen much of his younger self in Antonio, an earnest young man deeply in love. Yet a far better man than Malavolti had been at that age. With a much worthier object of his affection.

Or maybe it was because of his overwhelming fears for the child.

The dark knight's own brother, Alexander, who'd been born a year before Malavolti, had also been born too early, and he'd died within a few days. From what Malavolti had been told in his youth, the tragedy of the baby's death had irreparably damaged his mother. Weakened her. Physically and emotionally. Then a year later, Malavolti was born. So his mother's first child had come into the world only to die a few days later, and then, when her second son was born, she died giving birth.

These tragic thoughts haunted Malavolti all through the night.

It was a silent prayerful night, as he sat alone in the darkened chapel, close to a small wooden statue of the Madonna and Child, praying that God would give Maria and everyone else the strength to deal with whatever was coming.

At dawn, Zampa entered the chapel.

Malavolti turned, expecting the worst.

"Is the child dead?"

"Not yet, but she's dying."

The old monk sat down beside Malavolti.

"The child won't nurse, and it won't hold liquids. I'd be surprised if the child lived out the day."

"Has she been baptized?"

"Yes. Her name is Angelina Salvatore."

"Even her name is beautiful."

The monk nodded.

"Maria's awake. She'd like to see you."

"Now?"

"Yes."

Without another word, the dark knight stood up, bowed to the altar, and left the chapel. Quickly, he found his way through the convent hallways to the birth chamber.

Where he knocked on the wooden door.

Leonora opened the door.

The rising sun had filled the bedchamber, and Maria was standing at the casement holding Angelina and staring at the brand-new morning, at the distant olive groves.

Malavolti didn't know what to say, so he said nothing.

Maria turned and smiled.

"I've accepted God's will," she said.

"I'm not very good at that, Maria, but I'm trying."

"You've suffered too much because of that night in Niccone."

"Throughout my life, I've inflicted much more suffering than I've felt. I realize that now."

The young mother looked down at her sleeping child.

"She'll soon be in heaven where she'll pray for you and for all of us."

"She's very beautiful."

"Would you like to hold her?"

Malavolti was stunned by the idea.

"I've never held a child."

"I'll show you how."

Carefully, Maria transferred tiny Angelina and her soft swaddling blanket into the arms of the powerful dark knight.

Into the arms of her grandfather.

Despite Maria's remarkable courage, despite her acceptance of God's will, Malavolti still decided to conceal the truth about Lorenzo. He would discuss it with Zampa, and then, most probably, he'd tell Maria when her mourning was over.

He looked down at the little child in his arms.

She seemed miraculous.

He could feel her warmth through the blanket.

It was the most extraordinary moment of his life.

He wished that he could protect the child with his life, but he was helpless.

Finally, he kissed the child on the forehead and returned her to her mother.

Then he left them alone.

Later that day, the child died peacefully in her mother's arms.

Chapter 27

Assisi

Umbria: July 1320

Malavolti stood in the upper-church of the Basilica di San Francesco, amid the high pillars, beneath the soaring interior vaults. High above, through the beautiful stained-glass windows, brilliant shafts of diffused sunlight fell dramatically into the nave, illuminating the cathedral's twenty-eight stunning frescoes, each of which depicted a significant incident in the life of the Assisian saint. It was probably the most extraordinary basilica in all of Christendom. It was certainly the most incredible that Malavolti had ever seen.

No wonder the church had caused such a controversy when its construction began in 1228, two years after the death of the saint, on the day following his canonization. In both design and execution, the basilica seemed far too opulent to commemorate the life of the great saint of poverty, and it reignited animosities within the Franciscans between the minority Spirituals, known as *poverelli*, and the majority Conventuals. The indignant Spirituals felt that the order of St. Francis should not only be penniless, but that its primary church honoring Francis's legacy should be simple and modestly adorned.

Nevertheless, the Conventuals triumphed in the end.

In principle, Malavolti sided with the thinking of the *poverelli*, but he was still grateful that the church existed exactly as it was. It might not have pleased St. Francis, who was buried in a crypt below the church, or even Alighieri for that matter, but the basilica was truly awe-inspiring, seemingly imbued with the Holy Spirit. Malavolti felt certain that many lost souls would find or re-find God within this magnificent cathedral.

As for the dark knight himself, of all the treasures within the church, he always ended up standing in front of the same fresco. The one depicting the young saint offering his cloak to a poverty-stricken knight. Like all the paintings by the Florentine Giotto, the fresco was infused with a calm, understated, yet powerful spirituality, as the compassionate young saint, dressed in a simple blue robe, offers his cloak to an elderly grateful knight.

The fresco, like all of Giotto's work, was uncannily lifelike. Uncannily human. The much-traveled Malavolti felt that the Florentine's depiction of the human figure was without parallel in the pictorial arts of Italy, Rome, Jerusalem, or anywhere else.

The naturalistic aspect of Giotto and his apprentices was enhanced in this particular fresco by the landscape in the background which portrayed an Umbrian town amid rocky hills under a bright blue sky. Yet despite its realism, the picture was flush with the power of the spiritual.

The sacred.

For Malavolti, of course, the poor knight represented himself, reflecting his spiritual poverty. Now that Malavolti had returned to Assisi, the town of his birth, he'd come to accept the fact that Francis, his teachings, and his Franciscans continued to play a major role in his spiritual rehabilitation.

It was now three months since the death of his granddaughter, Angelina Salvatore, and much had happened. To the dark knight's astonishment, he was now the master of Metola. Before she died, Margaret had laid claim to her father's estate. It was her friend, Orlando Orsini, the canon lawyer who'd stood up in the Castellan cathedral on the day she died, who'd prepared the necessary documents and cleared the claim with both the civil and ecclesiastical authorities in Metola. Then, in Margaret's will, she'd left the estate to "my dear cousin Visconte," with the provision that half of its revenues should go to the poor.

Suddenly, Malavolti had within his possession what he'd once pursued by illegitimate means.

Which he no longer wanted.

Then there was the unsurprising news from Zampa that Marie and Antonio had been quietly married at Santo Paulo. For their wedding present, Malavolti gifted them the peregrine, Scone, that they'd grown to love so much. Given that they'd continuously spoiled the falcon, they'd essentially turned it into a house pet, and Malavolti smiled at the idea. After everything that he and his falcon had been through together, they'd both ended up much the same. Once they were fearsome warriors, now they were calm and peaceful.

Malavolti was currently in the process of bequeathing the Metola estate to the newlyweds. He had no use for the place any more, and he was convinced that the young couple would be compassionate landowners, devoted to helping the poor. How strange that Parisio's property and wealth would end up transferred to his abandoned child, then to his mercenary cousin, then to a young squire and his wife, who'd been disowned by her family.

Like Margaret.

As for Maria's family, before arriving in Assisi, the dark knight had made the long journey to Pisa to meet with Enrico Sorella. He'd done so under the pretense of a diplomatic mission from the much-feared German mercenary, Berthold Oetker. Given Oetker's reputation, Malavolti received an immediate audience with the wealthy nobleman. They met in his interior salon, where Sorella was accompanied by two Pisan guardsmen.

Malavolti wasted no time.

"I've come about Maria."

Sorella was shocked, then wary, then dismissive.

"I have no daughter named Maria."

The dark knight paid no attention.

"If any harm comes to Maria or her family, I'll come back here, hunt you down, and kill you like a dog. Then the wrath of Berthold Oetker will devastate your entire family and all your property."

Protectively, Sorella's two guardians moved closer, but Malavolti unsheathed his sword.

"Don't be foolish," he warned them, and they backed away.

Then he looked at Sorella.

"Do we understand each other?"

"Yes."

Suddenly, the dark knight swung his sword up to the neck of Enrico Sorella.

"Do you know who I am?"

"I do."

"Do you know the name Berthold Oetker?"

"Of course."

"Do you believe me when I speak?"

"I do."

Malavolti was satisfied.

He left the man's opulent residence, left Pisa behind, and traveled to Assisi.

Sometimes a reputation for violence can be useful, and Malavolti hoped that Maria would be safe from her father for the rest of her life.

As for Malavolti, his own life had changed dramatically since he'd left Mariconda three months ago. It was Zampa's suggestion that he make a pilgrimage to Assisi, and once he'd finally arrived, he was perfectly content. He spent his days and nights living with the kindly Franciscans, trying to decide what he should do with the rest of his life. He was still only thirty-six years old, in good health, and his seven long months of torment were finally behind him.

His war with the demons of despair was over. He had no foolish illusions that he was now a "good person," or even a "decent person," or that he was free from temptations or free from further trials, but there was no doubt that the ravaging demons had subsided.

Looking back, it was hard to comprehend, even now, what had happened during those terrible six months. In his earlier life, except for brief periods after the death of his uncle and the murder of his wife's lover, the dark knight had never been prone to feelings of despondency. Or desolation. Or despair. Or irrational fits of violence. Yes, it was certainly true that he'd always been a ferocious warrior, but within himself, within his interior life, he'd always been in control of himself. In control of his emotions. Even when he'd murdered François Lucan on the banks of the Rhône, he knew exactly what he was doing.

But for much of those six long months of his derangement, he'd been out-of-control. It was as if all the darkness of his past had imploded that night in Niccone when he woke in the damp field and realized what he'd done.

What he'd assumed he'd done.

It was easy to enumerate his problems: a motherless childhood, an absent father, the death of his father, the devastating siege at Acre, the homelessness he felt in Paris, the distant death of his uncle, the betrayal of his wife, the murder of François Lucan, the extermination of the Templars, the loss of his financial inheritance, his disillusionment with mercenary warfare, and his venal obsession with material wealth. Yet all of those things, he now realized, were perfectly insignificant compared with his willful rejection of his faith in the aftermath of his uncle's death.

The dark knight had become, of his own volition, a man primed to ignite into violence. Into hopelessness. Which finally happened in a drunken rage in Niccone. It was only his precious cousin Margaret, serving as the channel of God's grace, who'd calmed his rage and offered him hope. Later, when he'd deluded himself with foolish romantic obsessions about young Maria, it was again, dear Margaret, who'd surely helped him from beyond the grave.

During his eleven weeks in Assisi, Malavolti often wondered why God had been so good to him, since he'd certainly deserved nothing, but he'd finally given up trying to fathom the inscrutable will of God. The only thing that Malavolti knew for certain was that there had to be some as-yet-unknown purpose for him to fulfill in the service of God.

So he waited in Assisi, gradually reforming his life, hoping that God would reveal His purpose. Sometimes, even though it felt presumptuous, he even wondered if he might be called to serve the Franciscans in some way, but he knew the idea was ludicrous.

So he continued to wait patiently.

Thanking God for His many kindnesses.

Then his thoughts were suddenly interrupted by the sound of one of the Franciscans approaching him in the basilica. The young monk bowed politely, said nothing, and handed the dark knight a well-worn dispatch. It was a letter. It had been sent from Tomar to Berthold Oetker, then forwarded to Metola, then sent to Zampa in Mariconda.

It was a voice from the grave.

Chapter 28

Mountainside

Assisi: July 1320

The dark knight exited the Basilica and walked into the nearby cemetery. As he did so, he looked up at Rocca Maggiore, the high fortress above the town which swept the flanks of Monte Subasio. The sky was beautifully blue, the valley below was lush and green, and the day seemed to be one of God's most perfect.

Over the past few months, Malavolti had fallen in love with the little rose-colored town of Assisi. His birthplace. He felt that he could now understand St. Francis's special affection for this lovely Umbrian hill town. It was right here, of course, where the great saint had been born and spent much of his life. It was also right here in the Assisian Church of San Damiano that the famous red and yellow Byzantine crucifix had spoken to the saint, saying, "Go, Francis, and repair my church."

Which the humble saint had done.

There was much about St. Francis that Malavolti could now understand and even identify with: his dissipated youth, his love of troubadour poetry, his disillusioned military service, and his gradual conversion. Eventually, the saint would found the Franciscans, guide St. Clare and the Poor Clares, lecture Pope Innocent, preach to Sultan Malik el-Kamil at Damietta on the Nile, and even be rewarded with the sufferings of Christ's stigmata.

Malavolti had no such ambitions. He'd been a great and feared warrior, but a small man, and now he was fully prepared to do whatever seemingly insignificant service that he felt God wished him to do.

He glanced off to the east at the dense forest on the distant slopes. It was there, in the caves, beside the hillside chapels, that the Assisian saint had founded his order. It was there that the saint had joyously preached to the birds under the ilex tree, sleeping every night on a slab of rock hollowed into the mountainside. Recently, Malavolti had spent many nights in the same forest in prayerful solitude, and he planned to do so again later tonight.

Now that the objectives of his previous life were forgotten, Malavolti was searching for something new. As Dante had done. As Zampa had done. As St. Francis had done. Now he would try and do the same, feeling that this much-traveled letter might offer him some hope.

Some direction.

But first, he stared down at the graves of his mother Isabella Damiano Malavolti and his brother Alexander, both of whom he'd never known. Every day since his arrival in Assisi, the dark knight had come here to visit, and it was always the most peaceful time of his day. Finally, after a brief prayer, he sat down on a nearby bench to read the short letter from Portugal in the bright sunshine.

The letter, in a familiar script, was dated over a year ago and addressed to "My dear Visco."

> *Forgive me for not writing sooner. Having survived Morocco, I'm still a hunted man in France. Someday, I hope to explain my silence. At present, I continue to serve King Dinis in the continuing struggle. I've learned from various sources that you've become embittered, serving as a mercenary commander. If you desire another kind of purpose, I'm now based at Tomar in Ribatejo Province. I pray for you every day. Deus magnus est! – Augustus*

The dark knight placed the letter beneath his cloak, close to his heart.

He'd never been to the Iberian peninsula.

It would be a long journey.

S.D.G.

About the Author

William Baer, author of over forty books, has been the recipient of a Guggenheim Fellowship, a Fulbright (Portugal), a fellowship in fiction from the National Endowment for the Arts, the T.S. Eliot Award, and the Jack Nicholson Screenwriting Award. His various books include *Times Square and Other Stories*; *Advocatus Diaboli*; *Psalter: A Sequence of Catholic Sonnets*; *The Heretic*, *The Dark Knight of Assisi*, *The Gravedigger*; *Classic American Films*; *Luís de Camões: Selected Sonnets* (translations from the Portuguese); the Jack Colt mystery series (*New Jersey Noir*); and the Deirdre mystery series. He is a graduate of Rutgers, NYU, South Carolina, the Johns Hopkins Writing Seminars, and USC Cinema. He was also the founding editor of *The Formalist*, the director of the St. Robert Southwell Summer Workshops, and the film critic and poetry editor at *Crisis*.

His other writings have appeared in a wide range of literary, religious, and/or cultural journals including *The American Scholar*, *Chronicles*, *First Things*, *The Hudson Review*, *The Kenyon Review*, *London Magazine*, *Modern Age*, *National Review*, *The New Criterion*, *Ploughshares*, *Poetry*, *Quadrant*, *The Southern Review*, *The University Bookman*, *The Virginia Quarterly Review*, and *The Wanderer*.

He lives happily in a log cabin in northern New Jersey and loves pizza, books, sports, and chocolate.

Also by the Author

Catholic-Themed Novels by William Baer:

Advocatus Diaboli

The Heretic

Jacinta

The Dark Knight of Assisi

Selected Other Novels:

New Jersey Noir

New Jersey Noir: Cape May

New Jersey Noir: Barnegat Light

The Gravedigger

Novel

Murder in Times Square

Murder in Nashville

Annie Oakley Mystery

Mary Pickford Mystery

Central Park

Companion

The Sweet Science

Equinox

Selected Other Books:

Times Square and Other Stories

One-And-Twenty Tales

Psalter: A Sequence of Catholic Sonnets

Formal Salutations: New & Selected Poems

Classic American Films: Conversations with the Screenwriters

Elia Kazan: Interviews

Luís de Camões: Selected Sonnets (translations)

Writing Metrical Poetry

Conversations with Derek Walcott

www.ingramcontent.com/pod-product-compliance
Lightning Source LLC
Chambersburg PA
CBHW031444200726
48289CB00007BB/2219